"I admire the emotional openness, tenderness, and deeply uncynical tone of *The Handsome Man*, a novel-in-stories that feels unlike anything else I've read recently. Brad Casey's fiction debut is a gem that celebrates little blips of happiness and small, elusive moments of genuine human connection."
—Guillaume Morissette, author of *New Tab* and *The Original Face*

"*The Handsome Man* is about listening and writing, it's about the dream of youth, the desire to squeeze every last shimmering drop of life out of the present moment. It's about the vague and haunting ache that comes with loss and the people who make it bearable. From couches in Rome to frozen rivers in the Canadian countryside, the top of the Berliner Dom, and graveyards in Memphis, Casey takes you on an unforgettable journey through life's wilderness."
—Sofia Banzhaf, author of *Pony Castle*

"Brad Casey's *The Handsome Man* is an adroitly self-aware travelogue. There's an easy sensuality to his language, peppered with precious details, disarming humour, and insightful character studies rendered with unvarnished empathy. This book is gentle, sensitive, and full of longing, and reading Casey is like catching up with a long-lost friend for a big, cold beer."
—Rollie Pemberton, aka Cadence Weapon

"if yu want a book uv amayzing n brillyant prose short storeez that ar long in theyr implikaysyuns look no furthr ths wundrful book is what yu ar looking 4 ths is beautiful writing with full orchestraysyun n minimalist accents enjoy"
—bill bissett

"*The Handsome Man* is a testament to the strength and resilience it takes for people to create new paths of living, being, and belonging in this world. It's about a life given to adventure, chance, and intuition, and the various and surprising ways the world shows us care when we relinquish control. This book illustrates the struggle to create stability in this kind of life, exposing the magical and transcendent possibilities of living life on the edge without a long-term plan."
—Ashley Obscura, author of *Ambient Technology*

The Handsome Man

The Handsome Man

Brad Casey

BOOK*HUG PRESS 2020

FIRST EDITION

LIBRARY AND ARCHIVES CANADA CATALOGUING IN PUBLICATION

Title: The handsome man : stories / Brad Casey.
Names: Casey, Brad, author.
Identifiers: Canadiana (print) 20200194488 | Canadiana (ebook) 2020019450X
ISBN 9781771665858 (softcover)
ISBN 9781771665865 (HTML)
ISBN 9781771665872 (PDF)
ISBN 9781771665889 (Kindle)
Classification: LCC PS8605.A872375 H36 2020 | DDC C813/.6—dc23

PRINTED IN CANADA

The production of this book was made possible through the generous
assistance of the Canada Council for the Arts and the Ontario Arts Council.
Book*hug Press also acknowledges the support of the Government of Canada
through the Canada Book Fund and the Government of Ontario through the
Ontario Book Publishing Tax Credit and the Ontario Book Fund.

Book*hug Press acknowledges that the land on which we operate is the
traditional territory of many nations, including the Mississaugas of the
Credit, the Anishnabeg, the Chippewa, the Haudenosaunee and the Wendat
peoples. We recognize the enduring presence of many diverse First Nations,
Inuit and Métis peoples and are grateful for the opportunity to meet and
work on this territory.

Contents

She was glorious, burning. She didn't know yet that her husband was dead. We knew. That's what gave her such power over us. The doctor took her into a room with a desk at the end of the hall, and from under the closed door a slab of brilliance radiated as if, by some stupendous process, diamonds were being incinerated in there. What a pair of lungs! She shrieked as I imagined an eagle would shriek. It felt wonderful to be alive to hear it! I've gone looking for that feeling everywhere.

—DENIS JOHNSON, "Car Crash While Hitchhiking"

You're just someone out there in chains
You're just here on your own love again
—JESSICA PRATT, "On Your Own Love Again"

The American

I LEFT MY PARTNER, L, ALONE TO MOVE INTO OUR NEW apartment in Toronto because a few months ago we were together in New York and I took all my clothes off in public and I was in front of the American flag and the cops showed up and now I have to go back for my court date for this silly thing that happened out of love, this strange and beautiful thing, and I want to go back to L because I love her. I don't want her to be away from me, to be alone in the endless air in the nothing between the clouds and the nothing that rolls on and rolls on and on and on. To what.

There's a man a few seats up from me. He's handsome and I can't stop staring at him. He has slicked-back black hair, tattoos on his neck, his eyes are deep blue almost blond. He's charming the stewardess. She touches his hand, they share little smiles, secret smiles when she passes. I turn my head away when she passes and I hope she doesn't see me, I shrink away, grip the armrest of fiery death this metal box of wires in the sky in the nothing. The handsome man drinks his drink cool, his cool drink, and he smiles and everything belongs to him.

In secondary security at the Newark International Airport I see the handsome man again. He's arguing with a US customs officer who threatens to send him back to Canada. The handsome man says he's in New York because he's in love with a woman and she's here, he's going to her and he won't leave, he'll fight to get back to her and I love him now. He'll never win. I'm with him. Now I'm the handsome man. A customs officer calls me over:

"Why are you here?"

"I have a court date tomorrow."

"When are you leaving?"

"In two days."

Silence, no eye contact.

"Welcome to America."

It was July. It was July 6. It was wedding season, we'd driven through the Independence Day states of the northeast Maine and New Hampshire, in New York, New York with L, American flags were in bloom and us too. We found one flag afternoon, massive and shining of jewels in a Williamsburg park by the baseball diamond. Shining, L dared me to pose nude in front of it, the American flag, and we laughed and I did it because I loved her and America, the centre of the universe in motion, I loved her and now and a *click* of the camera, quick.

And then the cops came. One of the officers was young and disappointed in me like an older brother might be disappointed in me, like my actual older brother is disappointed in me. He looked me in the eyes and he said, "People have died for that flag," and he wasn't kidding and he was right too. He handed me a yellow ticket with a court date, disorderly conduct. I called a lawyer and she told me that up to fifteen days in jail was the worst thing that could happen, fifteen days and I'd never go back to America. The worst thing.

Back to now. I'm on a train, it's grey and it's raining. A woman sits next to me and she smiles and she smells like Halloween candy and she spends the entire train ride texting and I read my book, Alan Watts's *The Way of Zen*. He quotes Chuan Tzu, saying:

> *The baby looks at things all day without winking; that is because his eyes are not focused on any particular object. He goes without knowing where he is going, and stops without knowing what he is doing. He merges himself within the surroundings and moves along with it.*

Hmm, and we're at Penn Station and the woman from the train walks next to me into the street and there, in the New York street, she smiles and the sun is shining through a mist of the grey rising away into the nothing. A dreadlocked construction worker smiles too and her eyes are blue and she looks like she's high and I smile and we're all smiling now, smiling in America and tethered.

There's a jazz band playing behind everything, playing from a bar low beneath our feet like nostalgic non-existent 1950s, tourists gape their phones in the air aiming at their faces. I walk to 37th and 9th where a friend moved from Toronto to there, to here, and she has an apartment and she has a couch for the night and her name is Joy and when I find her building Joy buzzes me in and I find her apartment so many floors up, my feet echoing hello all the way up to Joy who hugs me on the threshold and she says, "Baby, I'm so busy, I'm sorry," and she has to leave and she puts the key in my hand, in my pocket, the key to her apartment, and she says, "I'm seeing this new guy, he's cute and tomorrow we can all grab drinks if you don't end up in jail!" We laugh. She offers me no coffee, no wine, there's a cat in the room and it's wearing a bow tie. It hides from me somewhere near, hello. I text L, I tell her I'm safe, soft words, I'm safe.

And it's night and I walk my entire life through Lower Manhattan, a feeling filling the air like if I stand here long enough something will happen. Something to change this. My phone rings in my pocket and I ignore it, I can't answer to anyone calling, no one knows I'm here. No one but L, Joy, and the state of New York and a woman passing asks me directions. She's looking for a bar called Local 138 and it's on this street and "I don't know it," I say, "but I can help you find it, the numbers go up from here," and she says, "That would be swell," her drawl the wind through the wind chimes. We're approaching 100s and we walk.

We talk about nothing, we walk together in the night. She's a student and she's new and her name is Mary Lou and she's from Needles, California, "The greatest wasteland armpit west of all of Ohio, which is also an armpit," she says, and the bar is warm and she asks me to sit. Six men fill the table beside us, they're watching a muted TV with the moving mouths of Barack Obama and Mitt Romney and they're drinking beer from glasses as big as their heads, their heads that play football as big as two or three people, drunk, all of them silent but the room somehow loud like a headache heartbeat pound in your ears and Mary Lou won't tell me who she's voting for, she says, "We're in New York take a wild guess, ya fool." She tells me about the price of apartments and the price of tuition and the price of transit, I tell her about my court date and she laughs. We're drinking flat beer in the heart of the world and she says, "So what do you suppose is gonna happen?"

"With what, exactly?"

"That court date of yours. You think you gonna win or you think you gonna lose?"

"I don't know, I have to leave it up to fate I guess."

"You believe in a silly thing like that?"

"I don't know. I guess I never thought about it too much."

"Well, you best get to thinkin. You can't just let everyone else in the world decide who you are. Who are you anyway?"

I don't know how to answer that question. I offer to buy another round.

"Lemme tell you somethin, boy," she says. "When I was just a girl, like a little one no bigger than one of them legs of yours, my Daddy brought me to a ranch, the kind with all kinds of horses. Big ones, lil ones, pretty ones, ones that'll bite you in half if you ain't careful. All kinds. He said I was gonna ride one of them for the first time. Oh boy, if I wasn't excited. I'd wanted to ride a horse since I'd heard one gallopin around in the big ol world just outside my Momma's belly, God rest her soul. It was all that I thought about. And here I was, just a moment away. It felt like a lifetime. And I remember that first horse right down to its yellowin crooked teeth. It was smaller than the other horses and spotted, it had long hair and looked like a pretty little girl, just like me. It looked like me if I was a horse. I was in love with her right away. I whispered, I'll love you always, if you let me, off into the air as if she could hear me. As if she could understand somethin like the love of a girl. And my Daddy put me up on that horse and he said now look, this horse is strong. Stronger than you. You gotta really dig yer heels into it, it won't hurt none. Just remember this one thing: The two of you gonna work in tandem now but only one of you decides what happens to you. And you're the one who decides which of you that is. You in charge? Or is the horse in charge? You're both big enough and strong enough to decide on that," and she finishes her beer and says, "Well, go on. Grab me another one then."

"But wait, what happened?"

"Oh it bucked me alright. Made a mess of me. I couldn't even look at another horse for oh some odd four years at least, goddamn. I cried and I cried."

"What happened in those four years?"

"Oh nothin," she says. "Well, somethin. But it's hard to describe. But shoot, everyone has a story like mine. Everyone. Everyone got a story like that one. You'll see." She gets up saying, "Well, I changed my mind. I gotta go, boy. Keep that drink for yerself." I ask her to stay and talk more. She smiles, says good luck, have fun, maybe I'll find you in Toronto someday. She won't. And she's gone. Quick as she came. I stay with another flat beer and the six silent men then wander. Wonder descending like nets in the night. I think of L. I text her,

thinking of you

then:

hey, I love you

She doesn't text back. It's late.

||

Morning. I wake, I learn to tie a tie. I thought of maybe a woman maybe I'd marry one day who would maybe want to tie my tie for me forever and then, outliving her, I would feel the need of her, of another, of any other as I stare at my now forever untied tie. How much I could lose, everything all at once.

The line outside the courthouse curves around the block of the great brick building of justice and scatters into the sleepy New York morning street, different than any other morning like a low longing howl. Here's what happens: I'm ushered through security, a metal detector, I stand in another long line. I hand my yellow ticket, the one the officer gave me, to a woman at a counter behind a plastic window. I'm told to go to courtroom #3. People fill the halls like we're all in high school between classes, everyone shuffling feet and slouching. I walk into courtroom #3. Pews on both sides like a church, mostly full. I sit next to a man who falls asleep and is kicked out of the room by an officer. I'm the only one, aside from the lawyer representing the hundred mostly men in this room, wearing a tie. All eyes look down complacent, mostly indifferent. The judge looks kind, her red hair to her shoulders, and she speaks and a fury of disappointment veils her face. I breathe. I think of Alan Watts. I think of Chuan Tzu. I breathe for sixty minutes and I'm quiet and the minutes pass slowly like an entire lifetime sitting there alone and after sixty minutes my name is called and I stand next to a lawyer, in front of the judge.

The worst thing that could happen.

The judge looks down and her glasses slide to the end of her nose as she reads from a file.

"So apparently you exposed yourself in front of the American flag."

She laughs. The officers around me all laugh, some of the indifferent men too.

The lawyer next to me shuffles. "Are you sure it was in front of the flag?"

"Oh yes. The officer was quite explicit in his language... I've never come across this before. I suppose it's lewdness but...I guess he didn't like the flag too much."

I want to speak up, I want to say that no, she's wrong, that I love it, that I did what I did because I loved it, because I was full of love, that I loved everything then and I was naked and I was strong and it's L who I think of and I think of Alan Watts and of Chuan Tzu and I stand there in my tie silent in the laughter like the wind.

"Hmm...we'll just fine you twenty-five dollars?" she says like a question.

I look to the lawyer next to me. He asks if that's okay. I say yes. I'm told to wait outside the room, someone will collect my money. A man in the hall asks me if I'm funny. I don't know what he means.

"You know, you funny or somethin? Like, was it a serious protest-type shit or was you just bein funny?"

I was being funny, I tell him. I thought it would make a good photo. He looks me up and down, he says, "You crazy."

I pay my punishment. Twenty-five dollars. I text L, tell her I'm safe. She asks when I'll be back. I say soon and no response.

Subway to Williamsburg. Men singing on the subway car, *if I have to beg and plead for your sympathy / please don't leave me girl.* I buy Edith Hamilton's *Mythology*. Mitch Horowitz's *Occult America*. Henry Miller's *Colossus of Maroussi*. This notebook. I'm in New York wearing a tie and I'm free and all is right with the world now, coffee. Stoops like altars on every building, I'm yearning now, this is what it feels like to want something, to worship something, I want to sit smoking cigarettes. I wonder that because I grew up Catholic all my heroes are dead or saints or both. I find a golden yellow sweater balanced perfectly on top of a garbage can and it looks clean and I put it on and it fits perfectly and this is it. This is my reward. I go back to Joy's couch, the empty apartment, and I rest. The cat with the bow tie hiding somewhere near, another life with me but hidden.

Joy comes home. She asks me how things went. I tell her, everything, and we laugh. Soon we sit together on the L train. A woman, drunk, looks Joy in the eye and she says, "Don't you look at me, sheeit." Joy looks away. The woman says, "I'll fuck you up, don't you fuckin stick your eyes at me. Fuck." Silent. Our stop.

We're in Bushwick and we meet with Joy's new boyfriend and he's as tall as he is wide and he's handsome as he is tall and he tells me about working in film now, how he was a truck driver once, "In another life," he says. "Strange, the shit life throws your way and it just keeps going on and going on and on and on." We go to a bar and we buy some cool drinks and we drink them real cool. The presidential debate plays on every television, Obama and Romney projected on the wall, on every wall, electric in the air. Americans gathered in America, all speaking America, more and more drinks. Joy goes home with her new boyfriend, I can't remember his name now. What even happened then but a lot of things lost. I go back to Joy's alone.

I leave in the morning. I don't remember if she said good-bye. Maybe there were tears. It was so long ago and there are so many things I'll choose to forget. How much was my choosing.

My final morning in America. As I walk to Penn Station slow and alone now, barely here, New York becomes one sound magicless and grey. Blond weave, hair on the ground, I barely notice anything now. Hungover, bad dreams: My best friend leaves me, my partner upset, I'm a jerk always. I'm a fool of the worst kind and the worst part is I romanticize it all. I sit waiting in the airport. I'm alone. Nearby an orthodox Jewish couple reading with their child, old ladies playing cards, people in suits, people on their cellphones, all of us walking to our airplanes, coming and going and leaving after all. The airport smells stale like the iron smell of seeing someone you love walk away with another person, another person who isn't you, who isn't the handsome man. I text L and she doesn't text back. Later she'll leave me.

The Hyena

I'M ON A MOTORCYCLE AND I'M IN OHIO AND I DRIVE PAST a field full of cows and it smells strong of cows, their cow smell steaming in the sun. I remember driving through Quebec with Laura, who drove me from Halifax to Montreal so many years ago, and I had a ticket for the train the next day to Toronto, in that time long past, and Laura and I drove then through a heat wave that sent all the steaming smell of cow wafting through the entire province.

We're two hours into Quebec and the smell before Laura asks, "How long do you think this smell is going to last?"

"I bet it'll be the whole drive, there isn't much else out here."

"My god, I hope not. Don't they grow flowers out here? There's got to be some sweet grass or some cedar or some lilies or something in this goddamn province that doesn't smell this bad."

"Nope, just cheese curds, milk, butter, and beef."

"Oh man," she says, steering the car with her knees, the TransCanada funnelling us all somewhere else, anywhere, somewhere sweet, and lighting a bundle of sage in her hands, waving it around the car. "You can have some of this when you get to where you're going. It clears the bad spirits from whatever room you're in. Just wave the smoke around."

"No bad spirits in this car."

"None. This car has been smudged by my grandmother's sage since the motherfucking day she bought it. When she gave it to me I kept it up, gotta keep up the traditions. Do you know where you're going to end up?"

"Not really. I'll figure it out when I get there."

"You don't have a place to stay, no job, no nothing when you arrive?"

"Nope."

"That's dope, man, good for you. How long you expect you'll stay?"

"In Toronto? I'm going to give it three years, I think."

We stay at a loft in the Mile End. Laura's friend who lives there is out of town and has some space and, "There might be other people crashing there," she says.

"Who?" I ask.

"I don't know, just other people."

That night each of us sleep on a couch in a large, mostly bare windowless room of guitars and mic stands and dirty couches and other people sleeping, the sound of strangers breathing in the night, the smell of mould, everybody stepping light. I don't sleep and in the morning Laura drives me to the train station and before I go she hugs me and says, "That's not how you hug. Where did you learn to hug like that? It's so limp." I say I don't know, no one ever taught me how, and she says, "You can't love someone unless you know how to hold them. Here, I'll show you," and she teaches me this: Give a firm squeeze, not with your strength but with your confidence, heart to heart, a light touch on the way out maybe on the arm maybe on the face, look them in the eye. "Don't hold on too long," she says, "you'll know when to let go." Laura says goodbye and she gives me a sage bundle and she says be good to this, it's being passed down to you from generations. It'll clear the way for love and everything good. Take care.

II

I remember now, ripping through Ohio, that for a long time I told people I'd jumped on the train in Halifax with a one-way ticket to Toronto, that I thought maybe I'd get off in Montreal, I didn't know where I'd end up and when the train pulled into Montreal I stayed on, I wonder sometimes who I would have become if I'd gotten off then, and I told that story so many times that I forgot it wasn't true and I believed it myself for so long and I don't know where the story got muddied and confused but it's three years later and I'm in Toronto and I run into Rienne in the street, a painter I'd met and become friends with recently, and I'm telling her this and if I remember right she says hey, I'm not doing anything today, want to get a drink? and I say yeah, I'm not doing anything important and the drink that we have turns into a lot more drinks and the day turns into the night and the moon is out hard I remember, big and new, loud as the sun everything blue and I don't remember much from the night but I remember meeting Matt, I remember Rienne falling in love with him that night, as soon as he walks past her like who are you and hi. How she looked at him, I'd never seen someone shine like she did then, shining like the most beautiful idiot alive. I remember his laughter blast like a gun, a hyena's face charming and sharp and menacing. I remember it being late at night, too late. I remember his tall and thin body dancing like he's dancing with the moon, dancing like a stripper. Still I remember him most at night. Rienne tells me a few days later, when they start dating, that Matt is new in town. He used to live in Brantford next to the train tracks, that he would get home from the bars downtown by hopping the train, that one night he decided to keep going and see where the train ended up and he ended up in Toronto and he just didn't go back.

Later Matt tells me he doesn't remember me from that time. He tells me this long after he does everything that breaks everyone else's hearts because he's a runner and he leaves and he breaks hearts and I'm still here and we're driving together in the spring in the car that his father left him after his father had died, only a week ago, the funeral is that day and Matt skips it, skips town and everything and he calls me and says I can't do it, I can't let go, come with me and I'm here and we're driving toward New Mexico. No, I think we're driving toward the Grand Canyon. And I tell him about the first time we met and he says, "I remember when we all went camping, me and you and Rienne and everyone else. That was crazy. How many people came with us that time?"

"Oh there must have been fifteen of us at least."

"Yeah, that's too many people, man. We're lucky no one died. Remember that night everyone did acid?"

"Yeah. We're lucky *you* didn't die, I was so mad at you."

"Ha! What? Why?"

We were all together, I say, all of us, and then Matt ran off without saying a thing and no one knew where he went and I didn't say it then but I was envious of him because I wanted to leave too but I was scared of I don't know what, something of the dark, the wild, of leaving and anyway, "When you took off," I say, "into the woods I remember Rienne had a real bad trip, she was so worried about you. She had this silk scarf that was black with red roses on it and she wrapped it all the way around her face, only her nose was showing, and she wouldn't talk to anyone. She just stood there by the fire, not moving, not talking to anyone, not making a sound."

"Hahaha aww, poor Rienne."

"I was mad that you hurt her. But do you remember coming back?"

"Yeah, that was crazy! I just needed to run, man, I took off into the woods, I ran until I couldn't run anymore haha it was great! I remember just stopping and catching my breath and being like, where the fuck am I? And I thought about Rienne and I was like, I think I want to go back to her. I remember just standing there, thinking about her and laughing. Then I walked back, I didn't even have a flashlight, it took me forever! I was, like, listening to everyone talking way out in the forest and moving toward the sound. Who was at the campsite when I came back? I can't remember."

"I was, it was just me."

"Oh man, yes!"

Everyone had gone out onto the lake in canoes and I stayed behind. I wanted to be alone, I tell him. "Then I fucking hear this laughter in the woods and this heavy breath like panting, I wasn't even sure it was real but then you came out of the trees like clawing your way through branches and laughing so hard, you landed in front of the fire and you started crawling around going 'oh man! wow!' and you were all cut up and bloody. It looked like you were wearing face paint and you looked up at me and you were laughing like crazy and I wasn't mad anymore. I was just glad you were there."

"Whoooa! That's crazy I barely remember that, yeah."

"I think that's the first time we ever really talked."

"But we didn't even talk though. We just sat by the water watching the moon. I remember that part really well. It was beautiful, man. Just sitting there together. Like magic."

We're driving into the Grand Canyon for sure because I remember thinking that driving into the Grand Canyon is like magic too, the kind of thing you can't describe in words or in pictures or in art, it's art all on its own. You have to experience it for yourself to understand. The Grand Canyon is like when you're a kid and sex seems like such a strange thing, like alien, and you don't understand why people go crazy for sex, why they get jealous, why they fight for it, why they seem like a whole other person when they're having sex, more animal, more present, so present they're possessed, they're mystical. You see it on TV, you see it everywhere, it doesn't make sense. Then when you're older you have sex and you think, I understand now, I see why. That's the Grand Canyon, the Grand Canyon is why, changing colour in the sun pink to orange to purple to blue and black again and a distance you can't describe, it has no point of reference. The Grand Canyon is chameleons changing colour covering the entirety of a million football fields in the middle of the ocean.

And we're there, Matt and me, standing in it, and we're standing over it now both of us wearing cowboy hats and Matt looks like the great cowboy of America, the one that people think of in the mercury-grey sunset, the one that doesn't exist, and as we watch the sunset over the canyon a man with a large camera asks Matt, "Can I take your photo?" A complete stranger. Matt says, "Knock yourself out," lighting a cigarette because it seems like the most natural thing to do now and the man circles us snapping pictures and he's changing this moment, taking away from the moment by capturing it, making everything two-dimensional but it's magic and I understand. We all want to touch magic, to steal it for ourselves.

It's early spring and the temperature drops below zero that night on our bodies on our tent set up on the ground still snow underneath. Our campsite is set up on a loop of camp-sites and our loop is called the Juniper Loop and we laugh about it and I don't remember why, we get drunk that night to warm up our bodies, to get tired enough for sleep. We play charades just to move our bodies to keep each other warm way out here. I hate charades, I say, Matt says so do I, laughing like a hyena in the Grand Canyon wrapped drunk in black Mexican blankets that we sleep beneath later, the two of us holding each other in a tent, someone holding me, our stomachs moving together, toward and away, his ass like a puzzle piece against me warm there in the cold of the metamorphic rocks of the Grand Canyon, sandstone and shale.

I think we drive out the next day, maybe we stay longer. I remember sitting on a spire alone in the canyon beneath a tree that looms over me like a protector, I remember writing in a journal, where did I put that? I remember throwing a rock into the great expanse like a spark, was that the day we got there? Or later? Then I remember driving out, the trains running with us along the highway. I remember the desert red like the fading red petals of a dying rose and we're there, then we're in a forest snow-covered, rolling up our windows. I remember being asleep in the back seat 3:00 a.m. waking up to a voice singing: *Jesus saves! Jeeeesus saves!* and a choir behind the voice then another man screaming about devotion and the headlights are bobbing up and down into a great black nothing and Matt starts singing too and maybe some of this is a dream. I remember getting to the Canadian border and the border guard saying, "Do you have anything to declare?" and Matt says, "What do you mean?" and it's light grey outside like six in the morning a great fog like a bubble around us and the border guard says, "Are you bringing back any goods?" and Matt says, "Just some loosies," like loose cigarettes and the border guard says, "Welcome back to Canada, boys," and waves us forward.

And that morning I remember looking at Matt driving through the grey bleak morning of Ontario and he shines against it like a bag of diamonds poured onto a thin sheet of tin foil and I wonder how it is that we, or him more specifically, are so alive and we have something inside of us like maybe beautiful men might have, beautiful men everywhere, and we are so alone in the world. We have no women with us in the world, no men either, the entire world full of women, full of love, and here we are together and I don't say it out loud but I marry him there, in that car, on that morning, an invisible cowboy hat of nostalgia hovering over our heads like halos or like ghosts, the smoke from the sage I took out that I'd carried with me all these years and I can't remember where it came from, I won't remember for years until long after someone does everything that breaks everyone else's hearts but to me only, and I light it then and the smoke fills the truck blended with the smoke of Matt's loosie hanging from his wet morning mouth, both of us laughing now like hyenas, both of us breathing in the two smokes, the smoke going into our lungs, becoming us. I'm coming down, I think. We'd dropped some acid a few hours before. How we didn't die I don't know. I can't remember why we went to the Grand Canyon, I can't remember much along the way, I don't know if he brought me because he wanted me there or I was the only one willing. He's my brother, my true brother I say to myself, and soon after this I don't see him for a long time like so long I wonder where he is, what he looks like now, the distance between us expands and he's gone and he's always with me and what's more brotherly than that? What's more brotherly than not talking. Isn't that what brothers do?

The Devoted

IT WAS IN OHIO WHERE I HAD MY ENTIRE LIFE STRAPPED
to the back of my motorcycle, a 1987 Suzuki Intruder I'd
bought off a guy and he was about my age, he told me he'd
driven it from Toronto to the Atlantic and back and that it
was sturdy, "Ol Janey," he said, "she's pretty reliable." I said,
"Janey? Is that the motorcycle's name?" and he laughed and
said he'd named it Janey after his mother, Jane, who died a
few years back and losing her inspired him to change his life
and he bought a motorcycle, he drove it as far as he could
and I said I'm sorry for your loss, are you sure you want to
sell this? And he said yes, it's time to move on, it's been a
long time since that time of loss and I wonder if it changed
his life, in fact. I wonder if it meant to him what it means
to me. I'm going now 110 on a turn passing a transport
truck on ol Janey and I think I might lose control, my teeth
clenched, my knuckles white on fire shaking the night air
revealing every next few inches of road new and unknown
and I see a sign that says *Imagination Station, Next Exit* and in
this moment where one funny move could kill me I think,
That sounds great, I wonder what that is, it sounds funny,
and I'm fine, still moving. I can't keep driving, it's dark now
and I've been riding the I-75 since Detroit where the 401

splinters into a dozen directions at least, stopping to eat, filling my tank with gas.

The highway going through Detroit is apocalyptic, shredded tires everywhere, chunks of road, chunks of bridges gone like they'd been spirited away or broken under pressure. At a gas stop, stretching, I get a text from Laura who I left a few days before and she's asking if I made it into the States safe and she tells me too that she's feeling better since I visited, says thank you. I'd gone to see Laura in Montreal before driving south because her boyfriend Étienne had moved out of the apartment they'd shared for three years and he'd left her, and something in me then said to go to her. The same thing had happened to me not too long ago, though I never needed anyone she might need someone and maybe I did then too, it's hard to say.

When I get to her I ask how she's doing and she says, "Surprisingly fine, it feels like a burden has been lifted off of me," and I say, "Oh!" like with surprise. We drink and through the night she talks about Étienne leaving her, this great love they shared gone now, as a good thing being gone and she's light and she laughs and we go dancing and late into the night I see her kissing someone in a corner and they're writhing there in the dark together, her and this shadow person.

Later I get Laura into a cab, her so drunk that when I look into her eyes I see another person looking back. The cab ride is quiet and Laura lies across the seat, her head in my lap and she says, "I'm sorry, Étienne," and I don't say anything and I pat her head and she mumbles in my lap drunk things and things I can't understand and I'm a little drunk too and when we get to her apartment and she lies down in bed I hear her say, "I think that I'm dead," and I say, "What did you say?" and she mumbles something, her eyes closed, and she says, "I miss you, Étienne," to me, as if I'm him. Then she's asleep and I wait there until I know she'll keep breathing, please don't go, and I find a couch and I fall asleep too.

In the morning I'm awake before her and I make a nice breakfast of eggs and fruit and toast, some coffee, and I'm eating it when she comes into the kitchen in a long kimono robe, all sparkles and smeared makeup and she says, "Did you make all this food?"

"I did yeah, here, have some," and I put it all on a plate for her and she says, "Okay, one minute," and she picks up the coffee and she drinks it as she wipes her face with a cloth by the kitchen sink and says, "What a night huh?"

"Yeah, it was fun," and I ask her, "Who was that person you were making out with?"

And she's quiet and she says, "What?" I tell her that she was with someone in the corner at the party and she says, "Um, no. I don't think so."

"What do you mean? I saw you."

"I mean, I don't remember much but I'm sure I'd remember something like that."

"What do you remember?"

She pauses and says, "I don't know."

"Okay, well, I'm pretty sure I know what I saw."

"Well, maybe you saw that but I don't remember. I'm pretty sure it didn't happen."

"Do you remember calling me Étienne?"

"Oh god. No, I didn't do that."

"You did that too!"

"Oh no. I'm sorry. Maybe I blacked out, I don't know. Maybe it's just all a big black. I wish I could throw this whole situation in there, just forget everything that happened with him."

And we sit quiet eating our meals and she says, "Do you ever wish something like that happened? Being able to forget all the bad things that have happened to you? You went through something really bad. Do you wish you could forget about all that? Like, how did you get through it? What was it like?"

And I want to tell Laura that people ask me this sometimes, that people I knew only in passing would lose someone and they'd write me, they'd ask me in bars and in coffee shops, cornering me at parties. They'd say you went through something difficult, how did you get through it? I never knew what to tell them. That something was missing inside of me now? That I could feel it, physically gone? That there was something dark there that grew? That I wanted it dead? Everything was embarrassing. When anyone looked at me I thought: This is all that they see. My loss. Every conversation would lead to this, every look. I feared that this was all that would define me. Even hearing her name caused waves of pain through me. I would hear her name everywhere. I saw her face everywhere. She was in every face. I would do anything to get away from what I felt. A day where she didn't cross my mind would someday be my only blessing. And I didn't want to forget her.

"You just move on," I say, but it's not true. It's something I learn to say to shut people up.

"What?" Laura searches my eyes, trying to find something behind them. Like something is in the way.

"You become someone new I guess."

"Not very profound."

"Well, I don't know what to say about that. How do you feel?"

"I don't know," she says, "I'm still making sense of it. Maybe I'll make sense of it later. Right now I'm happy to not think about it, you know?" and she laughs and we get dressed there in her big open empty apartment. Laura takes me to the top of Mount Royal under the clouds that are dissipating and we sit beneath a great metal cross covered in light, looking out over the city and we eat dark brown chocolates and cream sodas dyed pink and we find a pair of blue panties up there and a big marble like a cat's eye and a ring, golden and without decoration, and Laura says, "You take the marble, I'll take the ring." But what about the panties? I ask and she laughs and she says, "Neither of us is ready for the panties." We walk back down the mountain and it feels like she's okay, she doesn't need me after all. Maybe this was her needing me, just being here. Maybe that's all anyone needs and it's late in the day and I pack up my motorcycle.

I'm all packed, my leather jacket on, all fringe down the arms, Laura comes out to stand next to me next to my motorcycle to say, "Whoa, nice jacket!"

"Thanks. I got it second-hand." I point to a scuff mark up the side and say, "See this? I'm pretty sure that's all scuffed up from road. I think someone took a hard tumble in this jacket, like they fell off and slid for a bit."

"Whoa, maybe they died."

"Yeah, maybe. I hope not."

"Hey, I wanted to apologize. The other night was kind of scary for me. I don't really drink like that anymore, I don't know what came over me, you know? I know people who died that way. I could have died. I'm sorry, it wasn't a fair position to put you in."

"It's alright. I took care of you."

"I know, I appreciate that of course. But you don't know, I could have slept wrong and gone out in my sleep. Like, you couldn't have protected me from everything. It was wrong of me to put you in that position."

"Well, that didn't happen so let's be grateful for that."

"And I am. But you know, when I was a teenager," she says, "I knew a kid who died that way. I've been thinking about it all day."

"Okay," I say, "tell me about it."

"Well, I went to this party. I don't remember whose house it was but I remember it was in this gross basement, the floors and walls were all cement, there was one exposed light bulb hanging from the ceiling and a bunch of chairs in a circle and nothing else. I was seventeen, I remember, because I was in Mr. McArthur's class and he told us what had happened when we all got to school a few days later and he made a big scene about it, like he cried and got really mad, he punched a desk. It was kind of embarrassing at the time actually, but I get it now. I was a teenager and I didn't feel much but now, as an adult it's like, too many feelings. But this kid, I remember he got really drunk really fast and all the boys were laughing at him because he couldn't walk right and he wasn't making sense. It was winter and I saw him go outside without a coat so I found one and I followed him out to give it to him and he was leaning against the house with one arm and he was throwing up. Did you know that if you're freezing your brain tricks your body into feeling hot? You start to sweat and overheat and people usually take their clothes off before succumbing to the cold. People who freeze to death are sometimes found naked. It's like this backwards self-defence mechanism, your body doesn't want to feel pain anymore so it convinces you that you're feeling the opposite. But the weird part is that delusion pulls you faster toward death."

"I didn't know that."

"It's true. I think. I heard that somewhere. Anyway, he was making this terrible noise, it was dull like a rattle but deep and away inside of him. I put the coat on him and he looked up at me and he had this weird look. I've never seen anyone look like that. He looked like he was in a trance. Or like he was possessed. It was this mixture of terror and beauty. It's hard to describe but it was dark and it freaked me out. I felt hypnotized by him. I brought him back inside after that and didn't look at him for the rest of the night, I just couldn't. And then he was gone. He choked in his sleep."

"What was his name?"

"Honestly, I can't remember. And that's what's been bothering me the most. Like, what's wrong with me? Why can't I remember his name? It was a really important moment in my life and it feels like I'm looking at it through stained glass. I guess that stuff goes away eventually? But it wasn't even that long ago really. Maybe twelve years? Eleven years ago? Oh wow."

"That's crazy, Laura, I'm sorry you dealt with that."

"Well, you know, I didn't have to deal with much. Or maybe I did. I don't know. I guess I went to his funeral and I got to say goodbye. I remember looking at him in his casket. He looked different. Not better, not worse, just different. And I said goodbye, kneeling there in front of him. I guess that's important, having the chance to say goodbye. I got to do that at least."

And we talk a few minutes more, we talk about my route, what she's doing this week, when I'll be where I'm going and she hugs me and she says, "Take care."

I leave and I don't look back and I don't get far, it's too dangerous to drive in the night, through the big black, I have to stop in Gananoque to set up my tent before the sun again sets.

||

I can't keep driving but I do, there in the night of Ohio a few days later, and I go another hour on that shaking screaming thing in the dark because I'm not sure why. It's hard to justify the decisions I make now. I dreamed and then the dream was gone and I had to move, still, now, forever, nothing ends. I didn't ever know anyone wherever I was going and where was I going anyway and that was fine. At some point something inside of me said *I'll go south* and here I was, south, just fine.

I pull into a campground in Wapakoneta, Ohio, and it's dark and no one is awake here. Trailers and RVs but no tents, no motorcycles, no signs of life anywhere. I set up my tent in the dark and in the night. I wake up from the sound of thunder in the distance but no rain.

When I camped in Gananoque, just last night I suppose, I set up my tent in a secluded spot in the forest, twenty feet in, forest all around me, and the sun is going down so I sit near the water and I watch the sun from beneath the great metal bridge to America, covered in light, the sound of cars crossing, metal to the metal ground, the echo bouncing manic through time between the trees all down the river like an angry dog and I remember feeling nothing then, the numbness of wind and motor still locked inside of me and that night I wake in my tent and there is a man running through the forest, I can hear him, I can see him with my eyes closed and when I open my eyes he's there running toward my tent and I feel him and there he is, the black silhouette of a man standing over me looking down breathing heavy and I turn on my flashlight and there's nothing there, nobody, no one in the forest only me and I say fuck, fuck, shit, until my heartbeat slows and somehow I sleep again.

I text Laura in the morning and I tell her about it, about the man in the woods running and I say too,

I think it was a dream

and,

or it was my anxiety of being alone, it manifested itself that way

She texts back and says,

maybe it was a ghost lol

I write back:

don't do that, don't say it was a ghost

She writes:

you never know! some things are out of your control

and I say

like ghosts?

and she says

like ghosts

What is it, this thing running toward me in the dark from the long dead of history, it rushing into the present. What do I have that a ghost would want or anybody.

II

The Ohio thunder passes and in the morning I look at the weather report, it's supposed to rain just south of Dayton today. More south is where I'll be going. It's clear here today, all tomorrow too, and the road south is clear after this bout of rain that brings me to night so I stay and I wait out the weather.

And what do you do in Ohio. I go to a Bob Evans restaurant for breakfast, a great big warehouse of a place, and I think everyone here could be the president, all of them smiling white smiles, shaking white hands, there's a menacing politeness like everything violence behind their eyes. The waitress calls me sweetie and she doesn't look at me when she speaks, I eat half my breakfast: eggs and fruit and toast, some coffee. I'm reading *Piano Stories* by Felisberto Hernández, many worlds away, him long dead and buried somewhere in Uruguay, connected to me somehow and here I am so full, sitting here in Ohio and everyone is large, so large, so many large white presidents at the Bob Evans.

That afternoon I'm driving down a country road and I pass

a cornfield and there's a section of the cornfield along the road where there is no corn but there are five tombstones all in a row, some of them stones some of them crosses with the growing yellowed corn. I want to stop but I don't, there's a red church in the distance and I go to it and it's open, this church, and a woman in the parking lot sees my licence plate and it tells anyone who's willing to know it that I'm from somewhere far away and she says, in a kind colloquial way, "What you come all this way for?"

"Nothing much, ma'am," I say.

"You going inside?"

"I'm just taking a rest actually."

"Oh you should go in, honey, it's got all kinds of saintly things in there. They say there's more relics from the saints here than there is anywhere else in the world. Here in Ohio, can you believe it."

And she tells me she's from here but had never come to this church until today, something drew her in, she says, something in the air maybe.

"I haven't been inside a church in years," I tell her and she doesn't seem to like that and she leaves. I go inside and it's calm, I'm the only person here, no priest no congregation, just me and a room full of relics of the saints, cloth and blood and bone all of them long dead or misremembered or having not existed at all, shadows now, and I sit in a pew, here in Ohio.

A couple comes in and they sit in a pew in front of me and they both kneel and they both pray and there's something of the magic lost in being observed and I leave. I remember being a child, being told that if you're wanting you can pray, that God will hear you, and I prayed then that a woman would love me. I hid in our backyard behind the broken car that had always been there, broken and rust pink, grown over with weeds and with vines and grass and nobody saw me there, praying that a woman might love me someday and she didn't come for a long time and in that time I lost my belief in God and I lost my faith in prayer and I left and here I am now, having lost all those things and all that love we shared and God was there too probably, and here I am, sitting among the possessions of all these dead saints, seeing ghosts, running in a place where there is no pain or anything else for that matter.

Laura texts me. She says:

hey, I know I said I was okay but it turns out I'm not. I'm having a really hard time right now, can you call me later?

and I think what do I know anyway, I don't know what's inside of me either, all those things that I thought had died away coming back, everything rising, a shadow inside like a pair of blue panties left behind lying alone below the cross on the mountain.

Outside is warm and the air is humid from the rain just a few miles away. I can see the clouds in the distance, the grey between the clouds and the ground like a sheet, like a grey ghost falling clumsy from the sky. I walk around the church and there's a forest behind the church and there's a path leading into the forest and I follow the path. At the end of the path I come to a small house like a tool shed and it has two doors like an archway leading in and I open the doors and I walk inside the small house and inside is a little chapel, it's all 1980s-dream-memory-brown-panelled wood and six two-seater pews and an altar with the Virgin Mary, her eyes closed softly, face covered in veil, and an angel next to her holding an umbrella of lights and some of the lights are burnt out and black and they're all blanketed in pink, pink light, pink carpet, pink backdrop and the cross and it feels like funeral, the room smell of rose. I sit there and I sit for a long time and I think about devotion and I don't know why and I think maybe I'll make sense of this later. Maybe I won't make sense of this at all. Maybe I don't want to face up to this right now and that's fine, a shadow inside of me growing big. A great big black. Later I leave the little chapel and I walk the path through the woods back to my motorcycle and there's something on my mind now like a marble balanced perfectly on a ring. On my way back to the campground I stop at the little graveyard, all five graves in a row, the dead below me, the corn growing strong from their bones, the corn in this field, the field going on forever, far and away past the horizon. I stay there, the sun on my head, my body growing warm, the ghost of ol Janey beneath me soon big and warm and black.

The South

MY PHONE WAS RINGING AND I WAS STILL ASLEEP, HALF-asleep skin stuck to the leather couch, stuck from leather and sweat and my senses coming back. I've been sleeping on this couch in the sunlight in the warm room in my friend's apartment, a guy I barely know who I drank with sometimes years ago and people said to me then, watch out, that guy's no good and I run into him at a bar, he knows a guy, he says, and he meets his guy and we stay up at his apartment late and I fall asleep on his couch and it was good I ran into him that night, I think, because I didn't have anywhere to go, I'm wearing out my stay on people's couches. People I barely know. Me alone there now, somehow, how did I end up here. I peel my arm from the leather like the skin of another person, us sealed together in sweat, and it was nice, that moment, not knowing where I was or if I was sleeping or if it was another person next to me, a man or a woman really just any person or a couch. Everything comes back to me, I'm awake and I'm alive still and this is where I am and I answer my phone hello.

It was Laura's voice then and she said, "Hey babe, how are you?"

"I'm just waking up."

"Oh I'm sorry to wake you."

"No, it's okay. What's going on."

"I'm just checking in. Étienne and I heard what happened, I just want to see if you're okay."

I say thanks, Laura, thanks for checking in, and she asks about what happened and I tell her, everything. It was a hard time for me then, I came to figure out. It was a time of loss. I'd left everything behind and I thought then I don't need a thing in this world, no one owes me anything, I was never owed what few years of what I'd been given, I say, and Laura says, "Why don't you come to Montreal and stay with me and Étienne for a while. We'll take care of you." I say that's sweet, maybe I will and we say goodbyes and she says I love you and I say thank you, unsure of all of my love now, small steps.

I'm not sure what I'll do.

I think of that moment now, riding my motorcycle through Tennessee because I'm sweating so much from the sun and the heat and the leather and I have a lot of time to think and this is what I think about. There's a rider who passes me and he's going 140 at least and he's not wearing a helmet and he has a long black braid and all black leather everything with a big black flaming skull patch on his back and in his left hand he's holding a long black whip that is trailing behind him like a tail and he looks over at me as he passes and he nods and I'm giddy from nerves, what is this world where this man nods to me, how different we are, the most different. I'm a few hours from Memphis and the sun is high and I'm sweating, everything down here sweating, the ash and the oak and the willow trees green through the rolling valley.

My host, Jean, comes outside when I pull into her driveway, all the big white houses and abandoned storefronts, brown, train tracks and streets with no street lights, dark, it's the magic hour when everything turns rose quartz, warm orange. I smell like gasoline, Jean says, "Hi! You're a little late but I'm glad you made it." I say sorry, I had to stop a few times because the shaking from the bike made my hands go numb and she says, "No worries, you don't have to explain. Come around back, I'll show you where you're staying and then I have to go, there's sweet tea in the kitchen if you need it." We go around her very small house to a very small backyard and in that yard there's a structure like a small house, smaller than her own house and it's a wooden pallet about six feet wide and ten feet long and a roof made of tin and it's all walled in with a screen so thin you can see inside and Jean shows me the camera above it, says, "We have that camera there just in case anyone breaks in, it's always recording at night so don't worry," and I set down my things inside, next to the cot where I'll be sleeping tonight and tomorrow. Jean says, "Keep your things on this table, you don't want roaches getting in there," and I do and I say thank you.

"Just make sure to lock this door when you leave," she says, motioning to the door made of rotting wood, made of broken screen. "Can I trust you?"

"I think so," I say.

I'm so hungry. I walk through the neighbourhood. Everyone says hello, everyone I pass. I go to a store marked *Liquor* all neon lights and inside is all glassed in, I'm alone in a glass box asking for beer. I go to a takeout place and inside is all glassed in, I'm alone in a glass box asking for food. I bring my food and my beer home in the night, the night that smells floral like cinnamon laurel, loud pops in the distance, cars squealing tires, wet wood steaming popping in a fire. I write Laura and I say,

hi, I'm in Memphis I'm safe, how are you?

Laura writes me back,

hey, I just got in from work. glad you're safe, I'm fine things are fucked here

And I call Laura and she answers and I say, "Hey, what's up?"

"Nothing," she says, "work was hard today. I'm so tired. I just want to eat some CBD gummies and lie down."

"Sounds nice."

"Oh it will be. Soon, I hope."

"So what's up? Why are things fucked there?"

"Oh man. Do you have a minute?"

"Of course," I say.

Laura tells me about going out the night before, she met this guy, she says. "I really liked him, he was sweet. I was at Poisson Noir and it was late and I was dancing and this dude next to me just had this way of dancing that was like straight from his hips, it was really sexy. And he was wearing this long white shirt that looked like a dress and I was super into it and we danced for a minute then we talked a bit and he was really cool and we knew some of the same people so he seemed safe and he walked me home and we sat outside my place for hours talking. I wanted to ask him up but I didn't, I don't know. Anyway I liked him, he made me feel something, like I felt happy going to sleep. Then someone told me something really bad about him today."

"What is it?"

"I don't know. I don't know the details but apparently a few years ago he did something really terrible to this woman I kind of know. Like, he assaulted her at a party."

"Oh that's not good."

"Yeah, it's not. It's so fucked. I don't know. Everything I've been told is so vague. It sounds like it was something that happened that wasn't intentional. But it's not people's intentions that matter, it's what they do, right?"

"Right."

"I was thinking a lot about Étienne today. Our breakup has been really hard and I've been dealing with a lot of back-and-forth feelings about it but it makes sense. We drifted apart. He made a few mistakes in the end and that hurt but I don't think he intended to hurt me. I need some space from it and in time I think I'll forgive him for those mistakes. He's not a bad guy. But there's a big difference between making a mistake and breaking trust. Like, you can forgive a mistake but when you put your trust in someone and they break that? Some people don't come back from that feeling. Forgiveness doesn't even exist in that place. Like, did this guy make a mistake? Or is it something more insidious?"

"Does that matter?"

"I don't know! That's what's fucking me up. Like, is this a bad guy? He didn't feel like he was. The way I felt the other night, I haven't felt that in years. Not even Étienne made me feel like that when we started dating. But I don't want to put my time into someone who ends up being a piece of shit. I've gone through enough shit myself. I don't need to get myself wrapped up in this. I liked him, I don't know. Maybe I'm overthinking it."

"Are you going to see him again?"

"Ugh, I don't know. I'm still so new to this. It hasn't been long since Étienne left and I don't know how to date, you know? It feels like I don't know how to do anything. I feel brand new, like in the worst ways. Like, I liked this guy but what's being said about him, it's bad. If I hadn't been charmed by him I'd probably have heard this and been like fuck that guy and I would have ignored him. Aren't abusers usually charming? It all feels like a warning. Maybe I shouldn't be dating at all. The feelings inside me are so confused. I don't know. I want to see him but something is telling me I should stay away. Why can't this be easy?"

"I don't know if it can be."

"Well, ugh, anyway I don't know. How are you? How are things going down there?"

I say hey thanks, Laura, for telling me these things, I'm here for you whenever and she says shut up, I know, tell me about America. I tell Laura about my trip so far, the drive to here, all the things that happened, the man with the whip. I ask her what I should do in Memphis and she says you should go to Jay Reatard's grave and I say shit, why didn't I think of that.

A few years back Laura was visiting Toronto, we went to see Jay Reatard play a show. There was no slow buildup, as soon as he started playing the room became violent, the room screaming, "My shadow!" along with him, some kid jumped onstage and the kid got punched in the face and the crowd was pushing and rolling into each other like all of us in a storm and someone threw a pitcher of beer and it hit Jay Reatard hard and he threw it back harder and he screamed and he thrashed and he packed up his gear and he walked out on everyone and the guy who booked the show got onstage and he yelled, "Fuck this American! I don't care if they're from Memphis! This is the Alamo!" and he was screaming in tongues into the microphone the room filling up with chaos and nonsense and people were booing and people were cheering and everything falling apart openly, in public, all of us powerless. Except Jay Reatard, who left. Now I'm on my motorcycle and I'm driving to a graveyard in Memphis to find his grave.

And I'm sweating and I'm standing over the grave of a man I've never met and I'm saying thank you, I'm saying I'm sorry. There are no roses here, no decorations. Stone. There's a cave nearby with depictions inside of the stories from the Bible, a man and a woman holding each other, three men shrouded they're walking away, they all look like the man, they all look like different versions of that man walking away. Square and broken black cameras in the corners their red lights gone out. I go to the Wolf River, I go to the zoo, I stand overlooking the tiger cage, a memorial here too, tourists all around me. Everyone says hello and it's nice, it's nice here and later I tell Jean this, about everyone saying hello, everyone nodding. I tell her over sweet tea and she says, "You know, Southern hospitality is real but I'll tell you what, those people aren't saying hello because they're being hospitable. They're sizing you up."

I ask her what she means and she says, "Down around here people aren't too friendly to people like you. You look like a threat. Some kid got shot just a few days ago, right down the street not five minutes away and for what? Nothing. When someone says hello to you they're seeing if you'll say hello back. They're seeing if you're scared of them or not. And if you say hello that means you're friendly, they don't have to worry about you. People have to protect themselves. I mean, it still feels good to be smiled at, to say hello. So it is hospitable in a way I suppose."

It's night and Jean is making a fire in the backyard and it's so close to my screened-in room where all last night I woke from mosquitoes in my ear, branches breaking just outside and the fire is hot against my still sweating in the night skin and she says, "What brought you down here anyway?" and I tell her, I skip over the hard parts and I tell her I'm running away for a while anyway, on my way west.

"You got friends out there?" she asks.

I say no. Not in California where I'm going. I'll ride north to Victoria where I know some people, my only friend right now is Laura back in Montreal. I tell her about Laura and I tell her about the guy that she met and I tell her about what happened.

"That's really a shame," she says. "Women getting hurt left and right, all over, it's always the same. What do you think of that? Do you think you're much different from a man like that?"

I say I don't know, I suppose maybe, I try to do my best.

And she says, "Well, you never know what you're capable of so be careful. I've seen good men turn bad plenty of times. It's easy to be a bad man in the world we've been gifted. People will stand with you. You gotta work every day to be good. You'll be tested every day."

We finish our sweet teas and she goes to bed. I stay up at the fire, I message Laura to see how she's doing, no answer. In the morning I'm packing up to leave, I'm hungry, it's so early it's almost still night and there's a note taped to my door and it says:

Thank you for last night. If you want to come in and wake me up with a foot massage you can do that. —Jean

And it's strange, this note, I'm not sure what to do and I pack up my bike. I leave a note that says thank you, see you again and I leave.

II

I'm in Leland, Mississippi, I'm filling my tank and a man in a truck who had been driving behind me long enough for me to notice him, to feel like he might be a threat, he pulls in too and he comes over and he looks at my licence plate that reads Ontario and he says the thing that scares me most, here in the most south of the South, in the most southern of southern drawls: "Long way from home, aren't ya?"

"I am," I say. "You from around here?"

"I am," he says, "grew up here all my life. Never set foot outside Mississippi."

"That's impressive."

"Yup. No reason to leave, got everything I need right here. What brings you to these parts?" he asks, standing too close.

"Just travelling through, I'm on my way to Baton Rouge right now."

"Oh yeah," he says, following me too close into the store where I'll pay for my gas.

Inside I pay the woman behind the counter for the gas, seven dollars, not much to go on, the man standing close, watching me. The man looks to the woman behind the counter, says, "This boy's all the way from Canada."

"Oh," she says, and she looks at me like she's impressed but it's feigned, a superficial kind but it's nice anyway.

The man says, "You know, I collect postcards from all over the world. It'd be a peach if you sent me one," and he takes a torn old piece of paper from his pocket and he writes something on the paper and he hands it to me. It's his address here in Leland, Mississippi, and the paper is thin and browning and it's crumpled and at the top, written in quotes, in his handwriting it reads:

the mustard seed

and below that,

it's everywhere destroyed—delight / the mass of darkness is shattered

and I think maybe he heard this somewhere, maybe it's some sort of motivational quote and I ask him what is this you wrote here? and he says, "Oh just a little something from this thing I've been reading. Nothing much," and he says good luck out there, you'll need it.

II

Coming out of New Orleans the stretch of highway is all bridge over swamp, the I-10, the smell of humid mossy bog like sweat and it's so hot, I'm riding in only a T-shirt and it starts to rain not hard but it's like needles on my skin pricking away at my entire torso and no place to stop, nowhere to pull over. I ride singing "ow, ow, ow" a full ten minutes, wiping my visor clean of water, keeping distance from the cars that drive past, the wind off the transports pulling me close to push me away. When I can finally stop I put on my leather and the rain stops and I'm in Louisiana and I want to be home and I have no home now my stomach empty and thin. I think about Laura and about having told her partner Étienne once, one night we were at a bar when I stayed with them, stayed on their couch, I told him about being a kid and all the kids in my neighbourhood that were my age, they were all girls, about a dozen of them. I remember they came to my house one day and they all were playing in the garage with my brother, twelve girls and him, and from outside I could hear them all laughing and I wondered, what are they laughing about? They were wonderful to me, kind and mysterious, "I wondered about them a lot," I tell him. "My brothers would beat me up but the girls I knew, they were always nice to me." I told him this, I think, because we didn't know each other well and here I was sleeping on his couch, friends with his girlfriend, I wanted to tell him I'm safe, I'm a safe person and I remember him saying mmm hmm, looking away, taking a drink of his drink, putting his arm around Laura, her turning to us and saying, "Hey, what are you guys talking about?"

"Nothing," he said, "nothing important," and I remember this now and I'm embarrassed because what I said wasn't entirely true and I knew he could see right through me. I only said it so he would see me as something that maybe I was not. I did feel something for Laura and I didn't know what it was and I didn't trust it. I was desperate then, I could mistake and mould any kindness into something more. Maybe his instincts were right, I think, not to trust me. Maybe he thought I was a bad man and maybe I was, maybe I am.

I make Baton Rouge, afternoon, lots of time to rest. I park and I unpack and the people hosting me aren't home, it's just me in their garage rebuilt into a little apartment, little bed, little table. I need to eat and I walk to the nearest place that sells chicken, all fried chicken everything, I'm in the South, chicken and biscuits, great red flowers, red crape myrtle, so heavy and red in the glow of the great neon signs of fried chicken shops, the air smells everywhere chicken and red crape myrtle like lilacs like olive, a great sweet and salty smell of the South. I eat and I read *The Road* by Cormac McCarthy and I'm thankful for the break from movement, for a hot meal and a place to sleep. Some days I won't have that, most days. I write a little. I message Laura,

I'm in Baton Rouge, lots of strange things happening

My phone is ringing. It's Laura and I answer and she says, "Hey! Glad you're alright, I've been thinking of you lots. What kinds of strange things are happening?"

I tell her about the man in Leland. I tell her about the conversation with Jean, the note.

Laura says, "Wow. So you just left?"

"Yeah, I felt weird about it. I didn't know what to think."

"Well, I don't know, it's weird sure but she's probably just lonely and doesn't connect to people often."

"Is it okay that I feel a little uncomfortable about her asking me to come give her a foot massage?"

"Of course it's okay that you feel uncomfortable. And I think it was good you left a note acknowledging that you were leaving. But I don't know, I kind of get it, you seem like a safe person."

"What if I'm not though?"

"What do you mean?"

"I mean like maybe I seem safe but she doesn't know me and I don't know what I'm capable of myself even. Maybe I'm the worst."

"Are you the worst?"

"I don't know. I don't think so."

"Is this about that guy I met?"

"I don't know," I say. "How are things going with him?"

"Well, I talked to him," she says. "I asked around about him and what he told me seems to match up with what everyone else says. He was friends with this girl, they went to this

71

party together, they were doing some coke in a bedroom and things started going down and he thought it was all consensual but then she said stop and he didn't stop. He says he didn't hear her. He said when he realized something was wrong it was too late. She was different."

She pauses and I ask, "So then what happened?"

"Well, she left and I don't know what happened then. A mutual friend of ours said she was pretty fucked up for a while. She never outted him. He said he apologized and tried to make up for it. He tried to 'atone' for it, he said. He said they stayed friends after that for a little while but then she stopped talking to him. He said he feels remorse, like he understands that he did something terrible to someone and she's different now because of it. And nothing can change that, no amount of apologies or atonements. She's changed. You know?"

"Do you believe him?"

"I don't know. I don't know if he's lying to himself about what really happened. I mean, if you can lie to yourself well enough that you believe it then you can lie to everybody else. And bad people learn how to look good to others, how to look like they're doing the work without actually doing the work."

"Are you going to talk to her?"

"I don't know. I want to but I also don't want to re-traumatize her. Like, I think my situation doesn't need to involve her unless she wants to get involved."

"So what are you going to do?"

"I don't know! We kept hanging out afterward. It felt, good? I didn't feel any pressure to do anything. He was really gentle, which I liked. He's nothing like Étienne, which I liked. We ended up just hanging out and doing nothing and it felt easy. It felt like those rare times when things with Étienne were really good. But I didn't have to work for it, it felt natural. I liked just being in a room with him. But then when he left the room my brain was like, fuck this guy, burn him. There's no one clear thing to do, man. It's all fucked up."

"Do you trust him?"

"It's hard to say yes to that? I don't know if I can trust myself. It's been so long since I've been single, it's hard to trust my own feelings. I miss having Étienne around, I miss having someone there when I need them. Maybe I'm trying to replace Étienne and this guy is just there."

"You could meet someone else."

"Of course I could. But is it a never-ending stream of 'someone else'? It's hard to just throw yourself into anybody, like anyone. Even if they're the best, you just can't throw yourself into them without feeling like is this it? Is this the big mistake? I like him. I don't like the idea of him but I like him. I want to let myself be vulnerable. I might get really hurt here. I don't know what I'm going to do. Is it worth it to put your trust in someone knowing they could break you? That they did break someone?"

I don't know, I say. I don't know what's inside of people. I don't know what's inside of me. Some people don't come back from what I've felt. What I'm feeling.

When things feel lighter, more like laughter, Laura says, "So you going to write that guy a postcard?"

"I guess so," I say, unsure.

And she says okay well tell him Laura says hi, give him my number, he's probably cool.

I sleep and in my sleep I dream that my body is shaking, my body is moving, everything is black, I'm in a bed with the sheet covering me and I can't pull it off, I try so hard but the sheet won't move then it comes off my head but it's still there, another sheet, I pull the sheet off again and it's still there over and over the sheet over my head this thing between the world and me until it comes off and I'm awake and I'm panting like I just came up from underwater. It's hot, I'm sweating, the sweat staining this bed in this garage in Baton Rouge where am I.

‖

Texans drive fast, faster than anywhere in America, my motorcycle screaming through the afternoon, anti-meth billboards everywhere here. I stop just north of Houston, I'm in Livingston. I drive through the downtown, I pass a big white bus, a prison bus, every window barred up, the men inside look straight ahead none of them look out the window. I pull into Lake Livingston State Park to set up my tent for the night and the office is closed, a large white man in a large white truck pulls up, he says, "What you lookin for?"

"I'm just looking to camp out, sir."

"Well, th' office is closed but go ahead, set up your tent anywhere, pay up in the mornin. Best be quick bout it though, storm's comin."

I thank him and I drive into the park, there's no one here but me. No one knows I'm camping in these woods but me and a large white Texan in a large white truck. I message Laura,

hey, my phone is just about dead but I'm camping out at the Lake Livingston State Park, campsite #4. I'm going to message you again tomorrow, weird vibes here, just want someone to know where I am

and I turn my phone off and I set up my tent and I walk to the lake to swim, to wash my body. I haven't showered in days and it starts to rain and there's thunder and I can't swim now, I smell like gas and like sweat and now like rain too. I sit watching the storm and I think a lot and I'm really happy right now, which is a welcome change, and also something is missing. I remember the first night I stayed with Laura and Étienne. I remember lying on their couch in this new room in the dark. I remember that night hearing her and Étienne in the next room laughing, wondering what are they laughing about? Then it was quiet. Then it was the sound of skin on skin, a low moan. I remember the leather of the couch stuck to my skin, the sound of them together, the movement, the distance I felt from everything. What if it's just me out here, just me alone, always moving, always hungry for something everyone else seems to receive so easy.

I get breakfast at the Courthouse Whistle Stop Cafe early the next morning, filling my stomach. Everybody staring at me, no one says hello. In the paper there's an article on catcalling that ends, "Catcallers unite! Keep it up and don't let a transgender, feminazi, libtard or anything that swings left stop you!" I stop at a big-box store on my way out of town for some cheap food for the road, granola and peanut butter, there's a young woman working the cash and she's kind and she calls me sweetie and I want to tell her get out of here, get out while you're still young before they tear the kindness from your heart but I don't say a word. It's not my place. What do I know or anybody. I wonder what she thinks about me, I look like a mess dirty and frail, I say thank you. I turn on my phone to a message from Laura that says,

oh babe, message me when you're safe

I tell her I'm okay. I leave east Texas.

II

I'm in Austin now and I'm riding through town without a helmet and it feels a lot more sexy and a lot more dangerous and my eyes water from the wind and it feels like crying but the sun is shining and I'm sweating and I'm happy here, here and alone in the middle of Texas everything big, big as the moon reflecting light, a soft blue light down onto the house where I'm staying where we have to keep the doors open all day and night because of the heat and when I turn on a light twenty some roaches scatter.

There's an artist playing a show downtown, he's called Blackie, I saw him play in Ontario a few weeks before in a field at a farm and I'd never heard of him and I didn't know what to expect and we all made a circle around this man in the field on the farm and a heavy beat played and he took off his shirt and he beat on his chest and he screamed and he howled and the moon was bright that night too, it was a full moon, and a man who was choosing to tear himself apart in front of me and a whole field full of strangers far away from his home and from our homes too. He was beautiful, the most beautiful man I'd ever seen. I go to see him here in a bar in Austin where the bartender on the back patio is smoking as she opens bottles, no older than twenty-one, these are her glory days, shit. I remember the girl from the box store, I wish she was here too. I wish I could bring everyone I've ever known with me, everyone I've ever met.

Me and everyone and the man from Leland. They'd love this, all of us together and the moon too. The microphone isn't working and Blackie screams over too loud music and the beauty is gone, not gone but it's a different, more difficult kind of beauty tonight, people aren't paying attention, drinking their drinks. After the show I thank him and I say I'm sorry for the problems with the sound and he says, "Yeah brah, no problem," and he shakes my hand, my hand in his large hands and the same different, difficult beauty brings me to another bar later where I'm alone and I sit down and a woman starts talking to me, she says, "Hi, are you from around here?"

I say no, I'm from Canada.

"What brings you all this way?"

"Well, I just went to see Blackie downtown. Have you heard of him?"

"No, what kind of music is it?"

"It's pretty heavy, like it's more like performance art than it is music."

"Oh I wouldn't know anything about that. I'm from the country, I mostly listen to songs about trucks," and she laughs an open, full stomach laugh of the South.

And it's nice, talking with a stranger, being open being

charmed, and she tells me about Texas and she tells me about growing up in the country. She tells me about boys in the country how they're rowdy and she likes that. I'm pretty quiet, I say.

"I can tell," she says and asks if I want another drink. I tell her I'm driving, my motorcycle is just outside, maybe I shouldn't and she says, "Oh would you take me for a ride? I love motorcycles."

"I don't know, I've actually never had someone with me on the back before."

"Well shoot, I'll trust you if you'll trust me," she says. "Just promise you'll go real fast."

She's wearing my helmet now and I'm not wearing a helmet and it's a lot more dangerous and a lot more sexy and we're riding in the night and this woman who I've known an hour is holding me from behind, her arms wrapped around me, just above my stomach, my stomach feeling full. I don't know where I'm going and we drive through the strip, the lights are shining on us and the great state council looms up ahead, the bridge and the buildings, my shadow. The people of Austin lining up at trucks in the early Austin night, everyone drunk together, how they found each other, how everyone does, this man and this woman so different, giddy from nerves. It feels like they're waving hello and the night and the summer and the sweat and this is it, I think, this might as well be the first person I've ever met, this is the first person who's ever touched me, the sweat of her hands stuck to the leather of my great leather jacket, all of it wrapped around my body, my body tired and naked and full, a stranger, anyone, wrapped around me moving.

In the morning, everything comes back to me. I'm awake. I buy a postcard, it's a picture of a horse and a man and the sky before them bursting with something brand new, the sunset, everything, on fire, the lush plains he looks over. It's all a depiction, a longing of the past. The plains are a desert now. I ride through them alone, empty, the buffalo gone. All the flowers gone. Just me. In big bold cowboy letters it says, "Miss you, wish you were here…"

The Coyote

SUZANNE OPENS THE DOOR TO HER HOUSE, HER HOUSE surrounded by drought yellow fields and two horses at the gate, both of them staring at me, one of them jerking its head up and back as if to beckon me or to push away, the flies buzzing around him landing in his big blue horse eyes blue as the Roswell sky and I'm saddle sore from all day riding my motorcycle my 1987 Suzuki Intruder burgundy and hot as a stovetop burner red, my stomach empty, and Suzanne says, "You must be my guest! Nice to meet you, my husband is away at work all weekend. Take your shoes off I'll show you to your room," and I wonder why she mentions right away her husband being away all weekend and she leads me upstairs to the room I've rented for the night, the room with the big bed and the shower and the washer and dryer. I chose this room over every other because of the big bed and the shower and the washer and dryer, even paid more to be here over anywhere else because I haven't showered in a week, not through the Chihuahuan Desert, not through Marfa, somewhere farther back outside Austin I remember swimming in a lake but I could be wrong, my sweat like oil stains rainbow-coloured floating on the skin of the water and on the road, when a thunderstorm hit I watched it from under a bridge with a young Mexican family who smiled at me but didn't seem to speak much English save the husband who turned to me after a big bolt of lightning crack and we all went "Oooh!" and he said, "Big storm!" and I nodded yes and I smiled and they smiled back, the husband and wife smiling and their son who stared at me expressionless, me smelling like the musk of an animal, some gasoline mammal and lake water and all my clothes were sweat stained too.

I hear Suzanne downstairs making herself dinner in the kitchen surrounded by photos of her now adult children and her husband away, listening to a song I've heard before, something about little lies, tell me lies, I shower off all the sweat and the gasoline and the flies and I wipe the steam off the mirror and I look at myself there and I can't recognize myself now. Do I still only know who I was before this, just a moment ago, dirty having not spoken a word seven days?

In the morning Suzanne has coffee brewed and everything smells clean like lavender clean like coffee and I tell her about an accident I'd seen coming through southern New Mexico, through the two-lane oil-field road, through the desert surrounded by stacks shooting live fire up into the sky and there was a long line of cars that had stopped all jammed on the road and I stopped behind them and a helicopter flew so low up over my head and down into the highway of that desert not three hundred metres away, just beyond as far as the hill ahead of us rose and it landed there on the road. People were standing on the shoulder talking in small groups, shaking hands, a man with leather for skin and a cowboy hat of the same colour leather came to me with a bottle of water, said, "You're gonna need this, son," and I thanked him as he continued, "I used to ride one of them back in my day, how far you comin?" and I told him Canada and he laughed and when I asked him what happened he said, "Well, I'll tell ya, I don't know but my best guess is some oil boy worked a double overtime shift, drove ten miles of his hundred-mile ride home, closed his eyes for a second just to see how good it might feel. Now he won't be openin them eyes again." He told me this happens all the time, "Get settled in, could be 'til sunset to clean that mess up."

I walked up ahead to see what happened and what I saw was a large white man in a large white truck and the hood of the truck was torn in half and there was a semi truck not far off with its hood a little banged up too and a paramedic was talking with the large man in shock but alive, bits of truck scattered over the road, the desert shining now with treasures of chrome like jewels and people watching as another paramedic used the jaws of life to tear the entire front half of the large man's truck clean off and they were able to pull the large man out so careful, lay him out on a bright orange board and six men carried him, still alive mind you but like pallbearers to the helicopter and they were off into the sky and away and cars stopped on both sides of the accident as far through the desert as you could see, straight to the stacks shooting fire skyline. I walked back to where my bike and the leather-skinned man stood and he said, "That

85

man dead?" and I said no, he's alive, who knows how much alive though and the leather-skinned man said, "God bless him, I'll pray for him tonight. Y'all better do the same," and I said I would and I told Suzanne all this and she said that happens all the time out here, bad crashes on that road, too much, and she worries about her husband working there in the oil fields too and wishes she were back in Houston, "That's where my heart is," she says and she looks outside at the horse as she says this, the horse who'd beckoned me just one day before, now looking to the horizon himself, myself brand new now.

I'm not sure if I'll go back to Taos.

II

Santa Fe is a great brown beautiful spinning plate in the dancing gyroscope New Mexico and just beyond to the north are hills and mountains and a stream leads you up and up past *Danger: Falling Rocks* signs and they guide you sixty minutes to the dark side of a rocky gate like climbing a roller coaster and when you reach the top the Taos valley opens up like outstretched arms and the sun is setting and everything is lit like the setting sun through quartz, through crystal everything misty and warm and the dot of Taos there in the valley like a bull's eye and I pull over to the shoulder of the road because I can't see through the feeling in my chest that expands through my body like a blooming yucca and causes me to cry there in my motorcycle helmet moving one hundred. I drive down into the valley through the bull's eye, the sky growing dark, and move on

86

into Arroyo Seco, a village just past downtown Taos, up in the Taos Ski Valley.

It's dark now and the kitchen at the farm where I'm staying is all woofers and healers and people looking to be healed and it's noisy with breath and the dozen people sitting at the table all of them handsome and dirty most of them women they all stop and they stare at me walking in and I say hello and one of them, a woman named Valentine, says, "You're just in time for dinner, can I give you some food?" and I say yes but I'd like to sign in first if I can, to put my bags away, can I stay two nights? Valentine takes my hand like it's the most natural thing to do, leads me by the hand to a room, the hem of her long desert dress brushing my legs, she says with a softness and an ease, "You're welcome here, I'm your friend now."

I'm eating a meal of spinach and rice and spices, summer squash and sweet potato and it's the first good meal I've had in the days stretched out like months motorcycled on this road, the man sitting next to me a tall man strangely sad and handsome his name is Jorell, he says, "How long you staying? We could use another man around the farm to help us with the man things," and he laughs and I say sorry, I'd love to but I'm here two nights, I'm passing through on my way to California, I want to ride my motorcycle up Highway 1 up the Pacific, I want my bike to break down, to push it into the ocean.

"Just as good a dream as any," he says.

The next day we, all of us, Valentine and Jorell and me and everyone else go to the Rio Grande and we sit in a hot spring pool warm and silent and Valentine sits next to me and she puts me at ease as charming as a slow dance and three nude men nearby sing peyote songs and a sleeping dog there with them, Jorell singing too and when we leave, driving a dirt road late summer, a black dog from the bushes comes and runs at my moving motorcycle, head on and barking, and I swerve to avoid him and my bike falls and the dog runs off. The next day, what's meant to be my last day here, I bring my bike to a mechanic who says the damage will take a week to fix.

I stay in Taos, New Mexico.

Mouna owns the farm and she's a healer and she's in her seventies, her cabin hidden behind the farm sunlight stained brown decorated with tinctures and powders and scattered drying mushrooms and every morning she conducts classes with us all where she teaches us how to make toothpaste or how the lungs work or the origin of the universe. Some people are scared of her, she's powerful and she's very sweet to me and she lets me stay as long as I need, as long as I'm willing, I ask for a week and she touches my face and says, "We're all so happy you're here." In the afternoon Jorell and I mow her great green lawn shirtless drinking beer, our shirts wrapped around our heads, it's good to feel the sun on my chest, to breathe the dog air of fading summer.

We smell like cut grass and like beer and we've accomplished something notable, something like men might want to accomplish, and we go to the only bar in town, the bar lined with old men each of them like the man I met on the road full of leather. There's an old woman behind the bar and a ten-year-old boy and the ten-year-old boy takes our money as the woman opens our beers and we sit outside in the sun still sun drunk, Jorell says, "You know, there's something I've been thinking about," and I say okay, lay it on me and he whispers like a secret, "I want to be a hippie."

"What do you mean?"

"Like, you see how people are here. It's pretty relaxed. People take care of each other. I haven't been here much longer than you, I'm sure you noticed how weird everyone is. I'm coming from a whole other way of being, man. I'm learning a lot. And I like it, I think this is what I've been missing my whole life."

"Like what?"

"Like, I've just been learning a lot being here. Like I was defining myself by this role I thought I played and that role informed what I was doing. I wasn't defining myself by what I was doing, the role was informing what I was doing and I was defined by the role. I wasn't defined by what I was, what I is, what I be, the isness of being. I want to move toward that, I want to move past that. You know what I mean?"

"I'm definitely not following," I say, laughing a little.

And Jorell tells me, "Look, I used to work for the Globetrotters as a stage manager, real corporate stuff, a lot of pressure. I travelled all over the country," he says, "then I quit, got burned out from all the drinking and the moving and a different woman in every city. It just didn't feel like me. In the off season I got stuck in Santa Fe on my motorcycle, kinda like you, and I worked in this bar for a bit and Cormac McCarthy was a regular there, I served him a Scotch every damn day. And do you believe it but he told me, 'You should go to Taos for a weekend,' and I did. I came here and I didn't go back, didn't tell Cormac McCarthy I quit my job even. Let someone else serve him his Scotch, you know? He'll be fine," and he leans back in his chair and he takes a big breath like a big man and he says, "I don't need no more money no more. This is me, brand new." He chugs his beer and he admires the empty bottle like a jewel and gets up from the table and I'm alone now, I'm grateful and I'm drunk and Jorell comes back with another two beers and two shots of whisky and we drink them fast, me and this brand-new hippie man, hippie feather in his hippie hair.

There's a field full of horses near and when it's dark we wander into it, drunker than the leather men at the bar have ever been, him ahead of me laughing and falling into bushes stumbling after the horses who trot away and then I can't hear him laughing anymore and I hear coyotes howling like light snow falling on Christmas Eve night and I'm on my back lying in the dust and once I came here with a woman I loved and I'm wearing a sweater that woman I loved once loved and the horses buck and they bray around me spinning and dancing with the stars spinning over us and when I wake up it's darker still and I'm shivering, my entire body cold, my bones cold and it's hard to stand on my shaking legs and I stumble like a newborn horse feeling blind through the silence and the dust and the spinning, whispering, "Jorell..."

I find the farm and it's asleep, everyone, Jorell's there asleep splayed out like a starfish and I sit fetal on the couch in the main room near the fireplace and I'm humming like an engine that won't start, the largest blanket wrapped around me and the shaking slows, slowly the cold rises. I hear sock-foot footsteps and Valentine is there in pyjamas and she says in a whisper, "Hey, what are you doing?" I hum and I beckon her with my head, toward me, and I open the blanket and she sits there with me in the blanket and says, "Oh god you're so cold!" and she doesn't ask what happened and I'm thankful and she holds me and the shaking stops.

II

In a few days I'll be driving through Arizona alone again and tired and a storm will surround me the entire eight hours like a threatening doughnut in the sky, me in the hole in the middle, thunder crashing on every side, either chasing the rain or being chased and I'll suffer every minute of it, every healer in my heart. I tell Jorell about the man I saw when I was here a few years ago. He was a former stuntman and he was shirtless in a cowboy hat, jeans, he was throwing a football and thunder crashed on the horizon behind him and that image stayed with me ever since, it's so strange to be back here where that man stood more art than man. We're dissolving bits of peyote under our tongues and he says, "Maybe I'm that same guy now, maybe you're him for me." There's a blanket of anxiety lining the insides of my body, the back end mostly, the back of my skull all down my spine and it's coming down, it's dissolving like peyote under our tongues and I breathe in deep. We sit watching the grass which is a wonder and the dogs of Arroyo Seco that wander free are coming to us, we wave to them and we tell them and each other our stories about everything, we become the same person and the dogs become us too and Valentine finds us there and she has a dog with her and she says, "Hey, I found this dog in the street and she was really nervous, I asked around and no one has seen her here before." There's a tag on her collar that says *Daisy* and a California phone number too and we try to call the number but nobody answers and now Daisy is with us, the four of us here together. I tell Daisy, "You're welcome here, I'm your friend now," and her eyes are cataract old and they're kind and she's following me like a duckling. We find her a leash and we give her some water and we walk her down the street and we pass a funeral procession, locals holding photos of a young man wearing dark sunglasses, shirtless and track pants, beautiful and gone, the photos held facing the sky. Twenty men and women silent walking down this road, their faces like the sand and the stone.

At the cemetery Valentine takes out candles and she and Jorell sit in the grass chatting in whispers and she chants and I walk with Daisy between the graves. I show her the colourful sad beauty of New Mexico, every tomb a piece of art, every body artful, piles of fresh dirt and ribbons and red and gold and lavender like a birthday, no darkness, there is no misery here, no despair. A pickup driving past slows down to a stop, it drives in and through the graveyard and it stops before me and a man gets out and he says, "Daisy!" and Daisy smiles and she walks to him. He picks her up and he holds her and he says, "You found Daisy! Thank you! Where was she?" I tell him, everything that happened, how Valentine found her, how Daisy followed like a duckling after me, how we're friends now. He has tears in his eyes and he says, "She's getting old, she keeps wandering away. I'm scared I'm going to lose her."

That night Valentine and I watch *Casablanca* together in the house in the movie room. We watch it on an old VHS tape and we eat toast with peanut butter and honey and she falls asleep on me and I think I could be happy doing this for the rest of my life and the next day she's gone and Jorell leaves a few days later too because we're all here to give and to go, the sand and the dogs and the horses and before I leave Mouna tells me to close my eyes and she says, "I'm sending ten thousand rays of light through your body," and I feel something like fireworks exploding through my torso, like magic like warmth, something new flowing through my blood through my body.

My motorcycle breaks down again. I'm one mile into California, just beyond the Colorado River. I get a tow to the nearest town and in the nearest town I get a motel room and the town has no name and there is no grocery store here, everyone is buying food at the 99-cent store, everything is plastic and I call every mechanic within fifty miles and no mechanic will help me and it's a long weekend now, it's coming on Columbus Day, and the town is empty. I walk my bike into the desert behind the motel, I push it up a hill, up a dune, and the other side of the dune is desolate and there's one lush aloe plant and when I push my motorcycle in neutral down the hill, gone forever now, it lands in front of the only aloe plant prostrate like a believer. There is no water here. This is the end of the world and everything here is poison. The only person I meet is an old man in the parking lot of the motel and his stomach hangs so far out that he waddles and it's halfway in his pants, his belt holding his pants at his belly button his shirt tucked in and he's pale white and I can't see his eyes behind his dark sunglasses and the cowboy hat that looks fresh as a daisy in spring and he has a gun at his hip and he asks me, "You stayin here too?" and I say yes and he says, "Which room you in?" and I'm naive and I'm nervous because he has a gun and I tell him 207 and he says, "Hmph," and he walks off and he goes into his room, 107, directly beneath me, flies buzzing around my head, particles of sand and stone like every star in the California sky and I don't sleep that night. I don't sleep and I rent a car and I drive to Las Vegas and I get on a plane my body full of light and shaking like a sun that won't set.

The Elephant Graveyard

RIENNE PICKS ME UP FROM THE AIRPORT JUST OUTSIDE of Victoria and she drives me into the city and on our way a deer runs onto the road in front of us. I haven't seen Rienne since she left Toronto, since Matt left her and I spent a lot of time with her then. When he left, her body became a heavy thing, full of emotion raw and dark, lumbering heavy and wild where it used to be laughter and once during that time she came to my apartment, in the thickness of loss like humidity, and I made her dinner and she was okay and we drank some wine and she was okay and I went outside to smoke a cigarette and I smoked then because this was before I met the person who'd make me stop and then turn my insides into something else, something like Rienne had inside of her then, and when I came back inside I heard a noise from the kitchen like an animal in a trap and Rienne was on the floor crying, barely breathing.

"Put your head between your knees," I said sitting her up, and she did and when she could breathe she said, "I don't know what happened," and I said it's okay and held on to her, her body hot, a sickness turning red and I carried her into the bathroom because she couldn't walk and I ran cool water in the tub and I helped her undress and I helped her into the water and we turned out the lights just two candles flickering in the dark and she was breathing again. I had her hum with me, hum deep breaths out of her body and deep ones in and she settled and said, "Can I stay here tonight? Can we finish that wine?" Of course, I said, we finished a bottle of wine and then another and something of her came back, an upturned mouth, and she slept in my bed with me wrapped in a towel and wet from the bath and I wanted the laughter, I wanted my friend back.

Now Rienne is all tanned, all muscle, all yoga and redwood trees thick as an elephant and when the deer runs onto the road in front of Rienne's car on the highway she says, "Jesus, that scared the hell out of me."

"Yeah, wow, that was close," and I watch it run away from us and I say, "Look at it go though, wow. It's beautiful."

"What do you mean it's beautiful? It almost killed us."

"Wouldn't you want to be killed by something beautiful?"

"No, I wouldn't. Give me ugly every time. Are you joking right now?"

"I haven't slept in a couple days," I say, "my brain is firing all over the place. But I think I'm not joking? Is that something that scares you?"

"Hitting a deer? Fuck yes. Is this really what you want to talk about? I haven't seen you in forever."

"No, I guess not. Let's not talk about that."

"Listen, is there anything you need to do in the next few days?"

"I don't know, I could use a shower."

"Okay, well I'm bringing you camping up island. This guy I used to date, Eric, he needs to drive to Campbell River tomorrow so we're going to go with him. I want to bring you to Quadra for a couple nights."

"Yeah, I'm into that. Who is this Eric guy? Why aren't you dating him anymore?" and Rienne laughs and says I don't know, he's sweet, things still happen I guess. She drives me into the city, the two of us now, Victoria everything morning and she brings me to her apartment and she cooks me a meal and we drink some wine, all of her light like the old Rienne I knew and something different too, something tender full of flight, she lays some blankets out on the floor for me and she says, "You can sleep here tonight. I think I have a mouse by the way."

"So it'll probably crawl all over me while I sleep?"

"Maybe! He's nice though, he's clean, he's a friend of mine."
She says goodnight and she goes to her room and I lie there

on the floor in Rienne's living room and I sleep and I dream and in the dream I'm standing naked in a river and there are iridescent shining fish like I'd never seen before and they're swimming all around me in schools and their colours are neon blue, some yellow, some red, their bodies brush against mine and they're warm too and I see Rienne on a rock in the river and she's in the sunlight which looks warm and she's waving to me yelling, "Come here!" and she looks so happy there on the rock. I'm walking toward her and a black butterfly lands on my hand and it crawls across my skin and I admire it because it's beautiful and the butterfly stands on the web of skin between my thumb and my forefinger and it bites me, two sharp teeth through the web of skin. There's a sharp pain and I pull away and I try to shake the butterfly from my hand but it's still there holding on with its teeth in my skin and the pain then I'm on my back lying in the dark on Rienne's floor and the butterfly is there too and it lets go of my hand and it scurries across the floor away from me and as it moves it changes shape and it turns into a mouse and I'm awake now and it's the mouse, I think, a real mouse I'm not dreaming and the pain in my hand lingers and disappears like there's nothing there that hurt, after all, and the mouse stares at me from a dark corner of the room, its two eyes glowing red and I reach up to turn on the light and there's nothing. There's nothing there, no bite mark, no mouse, nothing.

II

I can't sleep. In the morning we have toast and eggs and

coffee and then Eric is there and it's still so early in the morning. Has the freshness of morning air ever made you feel sick? Have you walked so new into the world that everything is too present and you want to empty your stomach, your body turned inside out? Everything lost in the world of sensation? I walk to the car the way Rienne used to walk, heavy steps raw and lumbering. Does Eric say anything to me now? I'm barely here, he's handsome and he's large like a bear and Rienne looks at him the way she used to look at Matt but it's different now, a little lost like something learned and recreated and I sleep in the back seat, no dreams, the sun peaking somewhere on the horizon. Half awake I remember saying, "Oh, I forgot to shower," and Eric says, "Don't worry about it my dude, there's a lake on the way we can stop for a swim."

When I wake we're parked and there's a great thick fog all around us and I can see a shoreline and the water and I forget where we are and I ask, half sleeping still, "Is that the ocean?"

Eric laughs and Rienne moves her body slow upright like she must have been sleeping too and Eric says, "No, it's just a lake, we're right outside of Cumberland." I say oh yeah, right, and Rienne says hey, Eric, thank you and she touches his arm and she sighs heavy out her nose half waking. We get out of the car and we're all naked now because it's the west coast and the fog is mysterious wrapping around our bodies and we wade in the water together and it's very deep very fast and I dip underwater and everything down below is black, everything in front of me. I can barely see which way to swim to get back up to breathing and I'm awake now, I'm back. I come up and I can't see Rienne or Eric in the fog and I listen and I can't hear them and I call out their names and there's nothing, my voice echoing through what could be the middle of the ocean and fog forever all around me as far as I know, creatures down below in the black reaching up to pull me under.

Rienne and Eric both come up from underneath, from under the water, and they're laughing and the water is warm and it's nice to clean your body now and then. Eric swims away to the shore and we can hear him at the car, the car door opening and closing and Rienne is splashing me and I say, "I'm already wet, what is splashing me going to do?" and she says, "You smell bad!" and then Eric calls out, "Hey! Get out of here! Get!" and the car horn is blaring and there's urgency in his voice, everything between us stops and we swim to shore and he yells to us, "Get in the car!" and we're in the car now wet and warm and the car is already running driving us fast away our hearts beat like a drum, my ears screaming *bom boom! bom boom!*

Eric is laughing a crazy laugh his eyes so wide and he says, "Holy fuck there was a bear right next to me back there!"

"What?"

"Yeah, oh man holy shit," him driving still, fast, through the fog, "I got out to dry off, right? And I take my clothes out of the car and I'm putting them on and then there was this heavy noise moving toward me like it was lumbering and I thought it was you guys and I looked and there was this huge bear right there, like so close I could have touched it."

"Oh my god!"

"I know, it was fucked, I just started yelling and I don't think it saw me until then and it kind of jumped like I spooked it and it started running away, holy shit. Oh my god," and he's catching his breath and we're far enough away now that he pulls over and we all get dressed and he's laughing, he can't stop and Rienne puts her hand on his chest and says, "Oh baby, your little heart is beating so hard!" and she has him hum his breathing, big breath in, hum out. When he drops us off in Campbell River, at the ferry, still out of breath, he laughs and he says, "Well, have fun, be careful," and we all laugh because we survived something together I suppose, like some great cosmic joke.

At the ferry terminal the woman behind the counter sells us our tickets and says, "Gonna be a bit of a wait, the ferry doesn't leave for another hour." That's fine, we say, and Rienne says, "We saw a bear on our way here," and the woman says, "Mmm hmm?" We sit and I read a newspaper, I read about the mega earthquake that's supposed to hit the west coast some time in the next fifty years, plates of earth crashing slowly so quiet to explode to destroy Vancouver Island, the whole west coast. I ask Rienne on this beautiful day in our lives, I ask if she's worried about the mega earthquake and she says, "That's a dumb thing to ask, isn't it?"

There are piles of driftwood bleached white from the sun and they're scattered along the shore of the Salish Sea and I'm standing there on the driftwood balancing my body back and forth between the water and the woods. Rienne is in the water untangling her hair, there alone beneath the west coast sky, the sky like a great ocean all its own, the sixth ocean of the world: the west coast sky wet and full of fishes. Rienne steps out of the water and I throw her a towel and it lands in the water and we giggle "Oh no!"s, we walk, me dry as the driftwood, Rienne dripping water down the beach leaving a trail like a wounded animal, the wet towel draped across her shoulders, wet hair. There's something bobbing up and down out in the water and it looks like the top of a head, shining and wet like a skull, the skeleton of something, and I say what is that?

"It's a seal, I think," says Rienne and we stop and admire it because it's beautiful and it's a rare thing to see for us, us who don't belong here, or me anyway, and then we notice too, at our feet, that there is a dead seal at the mouth of the water, a perfectly round hole cut clean through, a pale blue and sudden and I ask, "Oh wow, what happened to it?"

"I don't know," she says. "It could have been eaten by another animal."

"What kind of animal bites into a seal like that?"

"I think there are only deer on this island. Probably a deer."

"Deer don't eat seals."

"Deer do whatever they want," she says, "deer aren't scared of anybody."

"Like the deer that almost killed us!" I say. "I bet it was the same one."

"Do you think that other seal is watching out for it?" Rienne asks. We look out into the water, the other seal gone now, gone or underwater. "It did a shit job," she says. "Fuck it."

Rienne loads my arms with driftwood bundles we'll use soon for campfire. She tells me the wood comes from lumber barges that pass and they spill the wood into the sea and the wood washes up on the shore and no one ever comes to claim them or clean them up, all of it tangled together, and technically the wood still belongs to the lumber companies, rain and bug full, and she says, "We're stealing so that's fun right? It's not often you get to break the law out here." There's enough wood here to build a home, all of it abandoned.

On our way through the woods walking back to the campsite there's something amber between the trees glowing and it's faint because we're losing the light of the sun, it looks like four ghosts suspended, glowing red, it's Christmas lights wrapped around a gazebo painted amber and it's decorated with photos and bells too, silent in these windless woods. It feels like walking into an abandoned house full of abandoned broken furniture or an empty church and there's sign inside that reads, *Leave what you have lost / Take what you must gain,* full of west coast optimism, like a nice naive kind, kind and hopeful. I have nothing to give. I don't take anything, I don't steal another thing. Rienne reaches into her bag, takes out a black scarf covered in red roses, she goes into the pocket of her jacket and she takes out her wallet and she takes out a photo of Matt, folded into four and worn with a couple years now and she says, "Fuck it," and she sets it there with the scarf among everything. She walks ahead and she doesn't look back and she doesn't take a thing.

Our tent is set up in a place where there aren't any other people nearby and the forest surrounds us on all sides like the circle in the middle of the dead seal. We open some beers and we start to build a fire and then the light gets low and it's just us and the fire and there are noises in the woods and it feels like there's nothing to say now and Rienne brings up Eric and asks me what I think and I don't know, I say, he seems like a nice enough guy. She says, "What was your scariest moment?"

"What do you mean?" I ask.

"Just campfire talk, bud."

"But what makes you ask that?"

"Well, I was just thinking about Eric and that bear. It's so funny, he's going to be telling people that story for the rest of his life. Has anything like that ever happened to you?"

"I don't know. Do you really think he'll tell that story for-ever? Don't you think he'll forget about it at some point?"

"No way. You don't forget something like that no matter how much time passes. That's the kind of thing that lin-gers, you know? Like the next time he's at a lake or walking through fog he'll be peering around, scared of running into a bear."

"You think it'll be something that repeats itself every time he's reminded of bears? That fear?"

"Well, I don't know, maybe he'll have other experiences with other bears and he won't freak out anymore. Like he'll go to a zoo and see a nice bear and maybe they'll become friends or something. But that first one, oh man, he'll always remember that first one somewhere in the past. As soon as he finds himself with his new buddy bear alone in the fog, he'll remember that fear."

"Well, I don't want to talk about fear, in the woods, in the dark. Let's talk about other things."

"Okay, what's your happiest moment?"

And I think about the first time I ate an oyster because it

seemed so gross when I first saw it and I'd never eaten anything like that, never wanted to, but I was with someone, her, who I loved, and she promised me it would be great so I tried it and I made a face but it was okay and then she laughed and I did too and the point is that I did something I never thought I'd do, had never imagined doing, moving through fear so simple but I don't say that because it's a hard thing to remember, that person having left, that happy feeling tangled up with all the feelings of loss, on a beach in the fog in the somewhere of the past. I say I don't know, I'll think about it. You tell me first.

"Do you remember when we went camping a few years ago and everyone took acid?"

"That was your happiest moment?"

"Well, part of it, yeah. You remember how Matt ran off into the woods and he fucking disappeared for hours?"

"Yeah, you were a mess when that happened."

"I was, yeah. And then he came back. That was my happiest moment."

"What do you mean?"

"Well, I thought he was dead! I was so fucked up and I disassociated, like I felt like I wasn't there. I was watching from above myself. I don't know if you've ever experienced that, it's terrible, like I couldn't do anything, I wasn't even there. I was beyond numb, I was like a ghost. But then when I saw him again it was like this great big breath flew into me and I was there again and he was alive and I was too, it felt like a dream. Then I remember I touched him and he was real and he smiled at me and he laughed and we were really alive together. I thought he'd never come back to me but there he was."

"He told me he came back because he thought about you."

"Well," she says, "where is he now," and something heavy moves through her, the context of the story changed now, everything different and she's silent. I try to think of something else to say, having maybe said the wrong thing, but there's nothing now, everything quiet and through the woods I hear something rising, a sound like a dog and the dog is barking and it sounds like it's at the end of the path, past the abandoned gazebo and on the beach in the night and it won't stop barking and it's an urgent kind of bark and Rienne says, "What is that?" and I say I'm going to check it out, I'll be back and I can hear her saying, "Wait!" as I move away from Rienne and the fire and onto the path and away and I keep moving past the gazebo now dark, the lights gone out, everything a dream.

I'm standing on the beach and it looks like an elephant graveyard in the night with the white driftwood and the shadows stretching into the sea. The air is dark and the barking has stopped, it's quiet like everything living holding its breath and windless. I walk forward. I call out Rienne's name but the sound goes nowhere as if I hadn't made a sound at all, she doesn't call back and she can't hear me now and no one can, everything black all around me. Is this a dream? Something nearby shakes and I turn my head to the shadow of a thing, two red eyes pop from the dark like the mouse from my dreaming, the butterfly and the mouse and the bear and I'm not ready to die, not by something beautiful or anything else, my eyes focus and I see the dark contour of a deer like a silhouette, like a ghost, the deer looking into me, me looking back at the outline of deer, then a blur in the dark and it's gone, the deer in the night full of fear and me too. I'm alone now and I hear the waves again like the faraway sound of cars on a highway, I can hear my breath, had I been breathing at all? All of it gone now, the sound of the dog and everything else, my heart like a drum *bom boom! bom boom!* the clinking sound of a seal or a skeleton in the waves. I hear Rienne in the distance calling my name.

I walk back to Rienne and I'm sorry, I say, for leaving you like that. "Don't do that to me again," she says, a little distant now. The rest of the night a confusion. Half sleep and waking. I'm laid down and I'm shaking, Rienne wraps me in a faux fur blanket, untangling the cold in my bones. There in the blanket something dark comes over me and I dare not speak. I look to Rienne, asleep by the fire, and see what looks like a tear running down her cheek. A tear from a dream of sadness or longing. Did she talk in her sleep or was that me? Was it singing? The fire burning out, the cinders popping in the exhausted wood, the sound like a chant singing *flesh, flesh, flesh.*

In the morning the tide is out. We find an army of starfish and oysters in the place where we'd swam the day before, everything different now. I take out my knife. I shuck an oyster there on the beach and I eat it, fresh and sweet as the Pacific, a living thing moving through my body there with Rienne and the bear and the dead seal and the dog and the deer and all of the starfish, all of them foggy and flesh and tangled together *bom boom! bom boom!*

The Movie Star

WE WAKE ON QUADRA ISLAND, THE SUN LOW IN THE SKY, Rienne making coffee on the camping stove. I pack up our tent. Neither of us speaking now. We walk to the road, Rienne ahead in the distance, we walk through the woods, the wet and dark woods of British Columbia each tree a thousand years old, one growing into then away from another and Rienne hasn't said a word to me all morning out of what I don't know and I haven't said a word either I suppose. We find two unopened beer cans in the moss of our walking on the ground seafoam, walnut brown and she says, "Should we drink them?"

"Of course," I say. "Let's shotgun them." And we do, giggling there in the place where we'll never be again, neither one of us. The morning passing, the moon somewhere too.

We're on the ferry back to Campbell River, I'm with Rienne, our backpacks and our tent. We smell like sweat and we smell like dirt and we eat from the ferry restaurant, the Coastal Cafe, because we've been camping eating toast and beans and packages of dehydrated wild rice adding boiled water to a bag and shake, our coffee instant coffee. We order overpriced burgers with cheese and bacon and mushroom and onion and a cup of coffee, probably also instant but it's fine because we don't know and we didn't make it, it could be anything, we're being served now after a week in the woods hot and hungry, we'll take anything now as long as it's given to us, as long as we don't have to try, leave everything to fate, let whatever has power have power over us, let it come to us whatever happens.

We take the Island Link Bus from Campbell River to Victoria. It's a long white van and everyone is quiet. Rienne sleeps beside me sat upright, the old couple in front of us and a young hippie girl too, the driver answers his phone and tells someone on the other end he has to make another trip today, he'll be home late and he'll bring almond tea from the city, "The kind you like…yup, the kind that turns the water pink," and ends his call with, "Love you too," Rienne asleep next to me.

II

I'm in Victoria for three weeks. I'm out of money. Rienne lives in an apartment building on Southgate. It's three floors, all white, everything white long and tall, baby-blue diamonds frame the front entrance of the building, blue flowers in the walkway of her home. Everyone is old and they stare at me like you don't belong here and I say, "Hello!" and they half smile hello, I'm sleeping on Rienne's floor.

Most days go like this: I wake late into the morning on the

floor in Rienne's living room and Rienne is gone to work. I tidy her apartment, I go for a walk down Cook Street, everyone is old and I go to a coffee shop and they don't know how to make an espresso and it's okay, I'll take whatever they have. There are chestnuts falling from high up from the trees, I watch as seniors crush the fallen chestnuts with their cars, they walk around great chestnut puddles, chestnuts fall and miss everyone walking on the sidewalk like all the luck of chestnuts, never hurt a soul. Easy. I go back to Rienne's apartment and I read, I watch movies, I pace and then she comes home and I make her dinner, I ask her about her day, we hold each other on the couch and we giggle until she has to go to bed again. I lie awake on the floor in the living room until I'm asleep, sometimes hours. So unsure.

This goes on for days, this passing time. Won't something happen, any single thing. I'm restless and I tell Rienne before she goes to work that I'm going to stay with another friend for a few days, starting tomorrow, I feel like I'm a burden to her, I'm occupying her space. I don't have another friend. I lie. I'll probably get a hotel room go further into debt. Rienne says, "Oh I thought we were having a nice time?"

"Of course we are. I am anyway. I don't mean that we're not."

"You're just feeling restless? That's all?"

"Yeah, pretty much."

"Okay, good. Because I like having you around. It's like you're my stay-at-home husband. I come home, the place is clean, you're making dinner, you ask me how my day is. Is that weird to say?"

"No, not at all. I've liked that too but this is your home, it's not mine. I'll have to leave eventually. Maybe it should be soon, I don't want to get attached to this."

"I get it. But as long as you're here this is your home too. And you're my pretend husband and the time you spend here is ours. This is our marriage, this is maybe the only marriage I'll ever get and you're not going to ruin it for me."

And I laugh and I say okay, that's okay.

Before she leaves for work Rienne says, "I understand if you want to leave, you're not a burden though, I like having you here," and when she gets home from work that night she says, "Hey, can you do something for me?" and I say, "Yes, anything," and she says, "Watch this really long movie with me, it's really long you might have to stay here through the whole thing, maybe all night. Maybe a few more days."

II

Then Rienne meets someone, a guy named Alex and I don't see her much now. She introduces me to him, he's nice, he's handsome, he's bisexual, he runs marathons, his body goddamn. I walk on the beach alone, I want to go home. I don't know what that means anymore, home. Rienne brings me one night to a party at Alex's house and his house is big and it's in James Bay and it's so close to the ocean you can hear the waves and the waves sound like they're singing, dying milkweed in the garden at the door. Alex tells me it's his mother's house, his mother a famous author he says, I've never heard of her, she's away on a book tour in America and he has the keys for the month. All his friends wearing J.Crew covered in tattoos, I'm wearing a sweater I literally found in the garbage.

The blondest woman I've ever seen, so blond she's translucent, so thin, sits down next to me and she introduces herself, Alana, says, "You're not from around here are you?" I say no, I live in Toronto but I was travelling before this, my motorcycle broke down in the desert so I had to go somewhere, here I am, she laughs and she says, "Why the fuck were you in the desert?" and there's something in her face I can't read, who is this person? There's a twitch behind the pit of skin below her left eye like she's making fun of me but no, I'm curious too, I want to know. She leans forward and she leans into me her hair the silk web of a spider, she's like a sexy ghost, flowing, I tell her everything about New Mexico, she laughs when I tell her about falling off my motorcycle, laughs so hard I think maybe she is making fun of me, maybe I'm a joke, maybe she thinks I'm funny.

And then an ocean of drinking. Where did Rienne go? Where is Alex? Everyone is loud and they're laughing and they're leaving now, Alana takes my hand we leave and we walk through the street lined with dead trees and we're at the water now, where am I? The people I don't know they all take off their clothes and their skin shines in the Pacific moonlight like they're coated in a thin layer of plastic. We're all made from a disco ball, whatever god made this moment plays disco from the dark water that pulls them toward and into it and this same god is dancing the dance of the moon and the ocean alone, slow dancing across the waves staring at me, doing a line of coke that is the approaching reflection of moon in the bathroom stall that is the ocean, this same god says this isn't for you, you don't belong here go home and Alana asks me, "Why don't you go in with them?" and I don't know, I don't know these people, they're her friends aren't they? Why is she here with me now? I don't know her. How did I get here? Where did Rienne go? Both of us, me and Alana, alone on the beach fully clothed. She says, "Hey, I don't know, let's go."

There's a tree in the street and its leaves are purple and black and they're dense like dark clouds and we're in them and we climb and in the tree we sing "Silent Night" in harmony, it's August and Alana tells me, "You know, I'm scared of heights."

"I didn't know that."

"It's true, now you know."

"Why did we climb this tree then?"

"I don't know. It's okay, it's weird. I don't know if it's about heights, really, my fear."

"What's it about?"

"Control I guess. Like one time I was on a private jet and I wished I was flying that jet so I could crash it into the side of a cliff."

"What were you doing on a private jet?"

"I'm famous," she says, "I have a bunch of money."

"I've never met anyone famous," I say.

We can hear her friends naked on the beach, them calling for Alana yelling, "Alana! Alana! Where are you?"

"They're like nymphs," I say.

"They're like dogs."

I tell her about driving to a lake with Rienne. Rienne and I went slow that day naked into the water, an eagle flew circles over us and the sky was the lightest blue I'd ever seen like another world entirely. A man showed up in a pickup and three dogs jumped out and one dog was so scared of the water and he picked the dog up and he threw it into the water and the man laughed a mean laugh like a sickness, he sounded drunk, Rienne screamed, "Hey! Man, what the fuck!" at him and the man laughed again but then she came out of the water screaming, "You should be ashamed of yourself! That poor thing!" and he saw she was naked and he saw I was with her and the man got mad and he left, he left the dogs behind even, the dogs chasing after the truck.

Alana laughs and says, "Tell me more!"

Okay, we climbed, I tell her, this tall cliff face and we found a long rope on a branch reaching out into the lake, a tree at the top of the cliff, a rope swing to swing into the water, and Rienne was so excited and she said, "I want to swing into the lake but I'm scared," and I gave her a pep talk, like, you can do this, I believe in you. Then when she swung out into the air, the air flowing down like water onto the rocks of the cliff below, she didn't tighten the slack of the rope so she dropped. The rope tightened and flung her upside down and the noise she made was sickening, all the air came out of her at once like all the life leaving her body and she landed on a rock in the shallow water. When she landed my first thought was she's paralyzed now, it's my fault, and I saw stretching out before me an entire lifetime of guilt, Rienne in a wheelchair, she'd never forgive me, but she yelled up to me then, the wind knocked out of her, her voice frail like an old woman now, "I'm okay! Ugh, I can wiggle my toes, oh," and I ran down to her and she draped her arm over my shoulder, I carried her out of the woods to the car, both of us naked.

"Oh my god!" Alana says, laughing even harder than before. "Was she okay?"

"Yeah," I say, "she had this big bruise all up her lower back for a few days after, we were lucky the rock she landed on was totally flat."

"I like that story."

"Thanks."

"I want you to tell me more stories," she says.

"Okay. What do you want to know?"

"I don't know. Will you walk me home?"

She takes me by the hand. Every tree in every street is bare. Had the tree we'd been in been bare too? I can't remember. Is she going to try to kiss me? She smells better than anyone I've ever met, smells better than any man or woman I've ever smelled. When I used to work in bars we had a big bucket and all the beer runoff from the kegs would flow into it, like the extra beer that got spilled or poured out, it sat there for days sometimes, and at the end of the night I had to carry the bucket full of stale beer back to the sink in the kitchen and I'd pour it into the sink under the bright lights in the quiet of the kitchen alone and I'd be so happy to be away from all those drunk people yelling at me. Working there felt more like babysitting than it felt like serving,

I wanted to serve people, I'd serve someone forever if I could, and the beer I poured out in the quiet of the kitchen smelled sweet like she smelled sweet, like a bucket full of stale beer sweet and alive.

"Are you going to kiss me?" she asks.

"I thought you were going to try to kiss me."

"Why would you think that?"

"I don't know, I just thought it."

"Do you want to?"

"I don't know, I guess it would be okay." I walk her to this big white house with an apple tree and a rose bush in the front yard both of them fully in bloom and we sit on the lawn and she tells me about Los Angeles and how terrible actors are and she tells me a story from set where this one actor had bodyguards to bring him everywhere and no one was allowed to look at him or say anything and he wore black everything, black sunglasses, he had his own separate everything, tables of expensive food he never ate, all of it getting thrown into the garbage and into the streets and she says, "I hate him but I want to be him too. I just don't want anyone to look at me ever again," and her world seems like another world entirely, full of death and otherworldly blue skies the way she tells me about it, and she hugs me and I'm three times larger now, three times strong, three women weaving on a loom, they say you'll love three people in your life: one you don't see coming, one that lasts forever inside of you, one to protect you from the rest, from death, all of them flawed, will this be the next the flawed love. She laughs and I laugh too then she's crying, her body convulsing against mine, I can feel her tears soaking through my shirt and they're hot against my chest, this strange moment, there's something familiar and not wrong exactly but something you'd never tell, something you'd never say out loud, just me and her and the moon, the moon saying go, leave now, who is this, where am I.

II

I'm back in Toronto. I'm working in bars, I'm working in cafés. I'm helping to renovate a house. I'm watching movies, I'm drinking a lot. I'm buying a bicycle, a black Nishiki road bike that costs more than I have, more than I make, I'm scared of cars I'm scared of sewer grates I'm so small out here. I'm avoiding certain places, I'm avoiding certain people. I'm distracting myself and I have no money and there's something missing deep inside of me, something that needs to be filled, something I assume everyone feels, don't they? I overhear a guy at the bar I work in, a man to another man, say, "It's like there's a woman-sized hole in my heart," and it's something like that, something, maybe there's room for a man in there too.

It's a few months after everything Victoria and I don't hear from Rienne now. She posts pictures of herself and Alex, pictures in nature, the mountains or the ocean or a sunset in the distance their hands reaching to the sky as if to say see this? It's glorious, it's all ours, do you not envy us. We exchange a few messages over a few months and it's nice to hear from her, what we shared gone, all of the west coast of me gone, all of it opened like a chestnut spread out across the floor. I'm in Toronto now. I'm restless and alone.

It's a few months later and Alana texts me, says she's in town. I don't tell her but I saw Alana in a movie recently and I forgot that it was her, the Alana who sang and who cried by the din of the ocean and as I watched, the woman on screen changed and she contorted and she became something new, something foreign, strange and comforting and terrifying at its core, something I didn't recognize. Have you ever had an experience like that? Where someone you know acts in a way that doesn't match up with the person you perceive them to be, they become someone new, unrecognizable? Everyone else can do that, I think, I want people to look at me that way for once. I want to become a projection, to be unreal and grotesque, something new. Can I do that?

Alana asks me to go with her to see her friend Josh play a show and I say yes and I go and she's there and she's waiting for me, leaning against the blood-red wall so cool and so small and alone. We're at the Royal Alexandra Theatre, this movie star and me, people staring at us under a ceiling of light bulbs like looking up at the sun from underneath the water and I don't know her really at all, she leads me up to the highest balcony high up in the theatre, her walking in front of me, she reaches back and holds my wrist and says, "This is terrifying, please be careful." There are signs on each side of the stage that read *Tragedy* and *Comedy*. I ask Alana what she's doing in Toronto.

"I'm shooting a movie. Honestly I kind of don't want to be here."

"Where do you want to be?"

"I don't know, nowhere. I hate LA, I hate the west coast. I didn't want to be in Victoria either, back when we hung out that time. I've never felt at home anywhere."

"Really? Nowhere?"

"Yeah, nowhere. I've never really had a home. We moved around a lot when I was a kid, I always travel for work, I've never stayed anywhere longer than a year. You just get used to everything being different all the time and like that's where I'm comfortable, I think, in not knowing what's going to happen next."

"Would you want a home?"

"I think about it sometimes. A nice partner, maybe some kids or something. It sounds nice but I don't think it's in the cards for me, honestly if it happened I'd probably kill myself and them," and as she tells me this the lights start coming down and the room starts getting dark and everyone gets quiet and the man behind us goes, "Shhh!" and Alana turns around and she glares at him as she says, "I'd probably kill myself and them," like she's saying it only to him and she keeps staring at him and she's like a large animal capable of death about to lash out at a much larger animal there in the dark as the room goes black as the singer comes out and he sings, "So free and too easy / Giving it away, giving it away." As the show continues, now and again I can hear Alana crying next to me, quiet, again and again.

After the show we go to a bar. A dark bar, I've never been. There's a man singing karaoke and his voice is bad and he's easy to ignore and he's made of the same stuff we're all made of, me and Alana and him all made of matter a million years old. There's a feeling about being with someone that everyone knows, everyone staring at you both, this man must be important if this woman is with him, this movie star, superficial and fake and electric exciting if you let it pull you into its dark and imploding fold. Where did you go, I ask her, what happened to you after we met in Victoria?

"I went back to LA the next day, for work. Honestly it's so boring there. Everyone I meet is such a bore, they're all trying to be seen every minute. They have no life except what other people think of them." She takes a shot and then another and she gives me one too and I take it and she says, "Maybe I'm no different. What have you been doing?"

"I don't know, nothing really. Just working."

"I bet that's not true. Your life seemed so exciting when I saw you last."

"Really?"

"Yeah, you had all these stories. You must have more stories, tell me something."

"I don't know," I say. I work most days, on Sundays I work a double making coffee at one place then biking across the city to bartend at another place, the best part of my day is when I bike through Trinity-Bellwoods because there are no more cars and it's slightly downhill and everyone is beautiful in their summer clothes, on their blankets, and for a couple minutes it's quiet and I don't have to try, I don't have to work hard. A few days ago I messaged a woman I'd met and I asked her out and she hasn't "seen" the message yet but that's fine, it's a good thing, I haven't felt strong enough to do something like that in a long time. The other day another bartender I work with said to me, "Savour this service tonight, we'll never have this one again, not this one in particular ever again," and she was joking, she was trying to tell me how unhappy she was being at work, the same thing happening to us all the time, every night the same but she was right. Everything good and bad would pass and not repeat itself, not ever, a million years would pass and still no one else would know this feeling, this exact feeling. I'm tired of trying, I tell her. I just want life to do whatever it wants to me.

We're singing karaoke together and we're drinking, an ocean of drinking because Alana has money, she's a movie star and I'm with her now and I don't have to try. And would you believe that when I was a kid, quiet and alone, I wished for a little sister because everybody picked on me and who would protect me more than someone who is smaller and is woman and is blood.

As I sing karaoke later, drunk and on the edge of forgetting, an old INXS song, I remember watching the video for it once, a man walking through a graveyard, so much longing, a woman at the bar boos me and she's screaming and I see across the room Alana is saying something to her and I can't hear what they're saying, what's being said, where am I. There's a bottle in Alana's hand and it moves toward the woman's screaming head and it makes a noise like *bonk* against the woman's skull like the sound of my little sister hurtled forward into the future protecting, then a whirlwind of hair, both women tearing at each other. I'm pulling Alana off this woman and her blond hair is streaked pink now and she's screaming and she's swearing and she tears at the world her face contorted, an evil thing shining a diamond in the night, she drapes her arm over my shoulder and we're running away now, us running bloody down the street under the stars that are the suns in other places, that maybe have died a million years ago their light still reaching out to us, things will happen and they're out of control always spiralling like a long many-legged insect curling into itself, spiralling like the great Fibonacci beast spinning the flaming wheel of fortune from the tip of its mouth, gliding, moving closer every minute moving toward us singing *oh isn't it fine, always being the same oh my.*

The Berliner

I MESSAGE NICO BECAUSE IT'S HER BIRTHDAY AND I SAY

hey happy birthday

and she writes me back immediately and says

thanks

and then a long, scrolling message. She had a heart attack a few months ago, she writes that she's fine and living in Rome now so I write back

oh my god

and I ask if I can visit. I've been moving around Toronto unsettled from a basement sublet to a room with no window then too north of Bloor, a large room with no heating and it's always cold and I try to write but nothing comes out but self-pity and I don't want that, that's not me and it's the longest stretch I've stayed in Toronto in as long as I want to remember. How long had it been? I don't explore beyond what feels safe. There are places that feel like walking through an abandoned house, there could be someone holding their breath, silent, around the corner. I need out.

of course,

she writes,

I'd love to see you. come see me

The airport bar looks like every bar in every airport, black faux-leather bar chairs, the bartender in all black everything, no expression, the bar a horseshoe, the cosmic horseshoe in the constellation Leo. A few seats down from me a man stops and he picks up a menu and he studies the menu with feigned interest, his eyes saying hmm and he glances at me like maybe he wants to sit here, maybe he wants to say hello but before I can say anything, before I can invite him to stay, before I can invite him to have a drink with me, as if I have it in me to do something like that yet, again, still so unsure, he leaves. We end up on the same flight together. Still I say nothing.

On the flight I read a book called *The End, by Anna* by A. Light Zachary and it's about a young artist and she creates purely from impulse with seemingly no influence. No pain has touched her, no complications. I have an old iPod and I can't add new music to it because it's not compatible with anything anymore and it only plays on shuffle because it's the only setting that works and the volume is low on the headphones I took from my work lost-and-found box when my boss wasn't looking and I hit Play and a piano song comes on, something low and rumbling.

I met Nico one of the first few days after I first moved to Toronto. How long ago was that?

I didn't know much about the city when I first got there, I went to a bar in Kensington because it's warm and it's dark and I'm in a bar in Kensington Market by myself and it's called the Embassy and a man sits next to me and he tells me I look like a doodle. I say, "I'm sorry?" and he says, "You know, like those dogs that are half golden lab and half poodle," and I say, "Ohhhh," and I laugh because I thought he meant something else, "a doodle," I say and he's charming and he buys me a shot and another shot and, "Some friends of mine are coming here for a birthday party," he says, "you should join us, you should be my date."

The bar gets busier and his friends arrive loud and drunk and smiling trailing confetti, sparkles, such beautiful faces in such a new world, wow, and he slips me something to swallow and he shows me off to them all saying, "Look at this doodle I found," him charming holding my hand through space. The man is dancing with someone else now, what is his name again, and I'm drunk and I see a light and I walk toward it and I say maybe I'm dying, out loud, laughing, alone now, I go off on my own and the light is an open door and a small room with four couches facing each other, all of them full of people and it's loud and the people there are talking and the words I don't understand at first, maybe another language, Italian I think, I think this is a VIP room, it must be, right? So I sit on the arm of a couch and I listen as they talk, all of them artists, they talk about their paintings and each other's paintings and they talk about Berlin and, "I wish I could go back," on everyone's lips and the woman on the couch next to me looks up and says, "Hey, what are you doing here?"

"Sorry, are you kicking me out?"

"What? No, why would I do that?"

"This is the VIP room isn't it?"

She laughs and says, "Where do you think you are? This is just a room. Are you here with the birthday party?"

"Kind of. I'm here alone but this hot guy thinks I look like a dog so he's introducing me to people."

She puts her hand on mine and she looks at me the way someone else would later, like she might lose herself, here she goes, only the look she gives is different it's hesitating and she says, "You definitely don't look like a dog, honey. You're good here if you're with me," and she tells me her name. Nico, after the Basilica Minore di San Nicolò. Where is that? I ask. Italy. Have you ever been? I haven't. Do you want to? I do. Is it okay if I stay here and talk to you? It is.

The Embassy is closing and we haven't moved from that

room and the lights come up bright and she says hey, let's go, and we walk into Chinatown still talking, just us now and she buys us a takeout container of noodles from New Ho King which is always open and bright and we sit in front of the restaurant with the neon electric New Ho King light of her face and the street lights and the drunk legs walking past and the way she looks at me, I think this is it. If this is all I get with this woman, this one minute, I'm okay with that. To brush up against this only. No one else will ever get this, as long as anyone lives, not ever this exact thing.

We walk past a church and the basement door is open and we look in and it's empty and there's a piano and Nico asks if I want to hear her play something, I say of course and we sit next to each other on the faux-leather bench and she plays quiet at first, something delicate and chaotic and free, the thick of the blue of her jeans brushing against me and I had a recorder in my pocket and she didn't know but I'd recorded her song then, that night, at the piano. Later, when she disappeared, I transferred the song to my computer, to my iPod, hoping to find her, to have her listen back to it as if remembering this thing that passed would change anything, everything that happened, this thing coming back to me and this is what plays for me now in this plane above the Atlantic. I'd forgotten it all.

I'm going to her now, so far away nearing the stratosphere above the layers of grey cloud above the ocean so far from everything, so far from that time. The pilot comes on the intercom and he says, "If I could get everyone's attention for a moment: if you look out the left side of the plane you'll see the northern lights, it's a good time to see them now if you want to see them." I'm sitting on the right side of the plane. I'd read that the northern lights make a sound, they make music. I want to see them. I want to hear them too. I won't be able to hear them over the engine. I stay in my seat. Something that I want is right next to me, ready for me and I don't go to it. I'm filled with a feeling like waking in a stranger's house from a shallow dreamless sleep and the TV is still on all static and she's gone.

||

I don't see the man get off the plane when we land in Berlin, I don't see where he goes. I have directions from the airport to the apartment I'm staying in but I don't understand them, I'm already lost. I ask a man at an information booth and he tells me to take the X9 bus to the U7 subway to Hermann-platz. I say ah, I see, danke. He sells me a ticket, he tells me, "Be sure to validate it as soon as you get on the bus." I don't know what he means. I should have looked these things up, I should have learned some German. I say danke schoen.

I ask the bus driver, "Does this bus go to the U7?" and he says a lot of things in German and I don't understand and he motions that this is my bus and I stay on, I get off at the wrong stop and I walk several blocks to the station, my backpack loaded with clothes, a laptop, my phone—I'm a moving target. On the subway there are so many people asking for change. I don't know how to say, "I'm sorry," in German.

A small young woman asks me for change and her eyes so blue they're blond, her hair is dyed bright red, she's wearing a leather jacket with anarchy symbols, a black dog black eyes is following her looking only at her, not me, not the others offering their hands, reaching for the dog, and I shouldn't be here, neither of us, the dog too and I give her two euros. I take out my notebook, I'm about to write about the woman and her dog, to remember, then I think maybe no. She's a person in the world not asking to be written about, here I am writing about her. I put my notebook away. I want to remember something. I want to make a document of this so I can remember, I'm forgetting too often.

I walk into Neukölln. I walk down Sonnenallee. It's morning and the city is lumbering awake, everywhere the air grey blue. Arabic men gathered in groups all of them talking together all of them at once, young women walking with young men, older women walking with children, so many groups of men, Turkish coffee being poured in the street into delicate gold, plastic golden cups. When I met Nico and she pulled me from the million faces of a million bars, we walked through the city into a morning like this. The light coming slowly and she brings me around the back of a house in Kensington and we walk up the fire escape and she says, "You have to be quiet, my roommates are probably asleep," and we're quiet onto the roof of this building and we can see the whole market from here, we lie on the black cool roof holding each other and my body is two times its size now and shaking and I'm warm now from the heat of her body and coming down and this is why I came here, I think. It wasn't though. Her breathing slows and she closes her eyes and for a minute everything goes quiet and she jolts awake as if from a dream, a bad dream where you're falling and you hit and she says, "Oh wow, sorry. I'm tired, you should go home I think," so I do because she asks me to I'm full of something new and here I go goodbye, a kiss on the top of her head and I go. A few hours later my phone rings, me slipping in and out of sleep, blood in my veins, and it's her, it's Nico and she says, "Sorry, I couldn't stop thinking about you." I hadn't stopped thinking about her.

"I shouldn't have asked you to leave," she says. Can I call you in a week? You can call me any time. Tomorrow? Hang up and call me back right away. I'd like to see you again. I'd like to see you again.

I don't hear from her again. I thought about her now and then, walking through Toronto, hoping she'd be there turning some corner I turned. Every time I walk past the Embassy bar she comes into my mind like a figure falling through a dream. Now I'm in Berlin and the sun is rising and I'm happy to be anywhere but Toronto, haven't slept in days, so tired I feel electric my body heavy with hormones flowing through me keeping me awake moving as if the world moves around me, here I am floating in one place goddamn.

I get to my host's apartment and my host is from Australia and she tells me all the good local bars and all the good local restaurants and she invites me to a sex party too. "I'm going with a couple friends. You can join but only if you're keen on something like that," she says. "Sounds cool though, right?" I say yes but I need a coffee so bad and she tells me all the good local cafés and I leave my bags, I'm not a target now, I can't remember her name. I feel free from something. I go to a café called k-fetisch and the man from the airport in Toronto, the man from my flight, is there and when he sees me he smiles and I say hey, this is weird but I think we were on the same flight a few days ago? and he says, "Yeah, I remember you, that's so funny. What are you doing here?" I tell him a little but I don't mention Nico and he tells me his name his name is Amir and he's here visiting friends, "I'm going to meet them now but they don't have much time for me. They're going to some sex party but I don't know if I'm into it. I have a couple days off, tomorrow and the next day. Want to go to a museum or something?"

That night I go to a bar near where I'm staying and it's called O.T. Raum and I sit at the bar and I drink a two-euro beer which is three dollars for me and I read *Coeur de Lion* by Ariana Reines and there's a dog there and its name is Georgie and it's the bartender's dog, he says to me, "Don't mind him, he's getting older. He's getting bolder, not a care in the world," he's Australian too and the dog lies in the middle of everything, its tail beating against the floor. Later, somewhere between six and eight euros which is nine to twelve dollars the bartender yells to the bar, "Hey, where's Georgie gone?" Someone points outside and says, "Is that him?" and there he is, standing in the middle of the street tail waving, cars slowing down slowly going around him and the bartender stops serving, stops the entire bar, everything, everyone stops everywhere now and he runs outside and he leads Georgie back inside by the collar, he points and he scolds and Georgie wags his tail, looks up at the man oblivious, joyful while the man tells him don't do that, Georgie, stay here will ya? Georgie's tail wagging the whole time. "He looks at you like he really loves you," someone says to the bartender.

"Is that love?" he laughs.

II

The next day I'm following Amir through a museum on Museum Island and it feels like we're old friends, the shared experience of being an alien, everything new, us together. We stand in front of a painting of a mermaid and her eyes shine a psychedelic happiness staring into the sky and I think of how I felt that once, the psychedelic happiness, how it was pulled away. We stand in front of the Ishtar Gate, a great bright blue wall excavated in Iran and brought here to Berlin and Amir tells me his parents are Iranian and he tells me he's wanted to see this wall for years and his eyes light up and he's gone now, lost in it now. He asks me, "What do you think compelled them to make this wall like this, all bright blue and gold?" I say I don't know, maybe there's an information sheet here and he says, "No, I mean like did they make it to claim ownership over something beautiful? Was it a show of power? Why did we have to dig it back up after it's gone, to put it on display for the enjoyment of strangers? In another country, untethered from its roots. I bet it was so much work to make this, I bet a lot of people got hurt making it."

We get a drink at a bar where an old man stands nude on a stage holding a mirror and he's staring at the back wall expressionless. No one pays him much attention. Amir tells me he's recently begun to date a man, that he doesn't know how to come out to his parents, to his friends, that he's kept his relationship secret. "Don't tell," he says, "this is between you and me now," and he smiles and we go to another bar called SilverFuture and it's a gay bar and his eyes light up again, different from before, this time like the mermaid from the painting and I'm here too, bright. Amir's friend comes, joins us for a drink and his friend is named Jana and she's beautiful and her voice is soft and her hair is long and this is how I meet Jana, full of a kind of wonder, drunk and twisted into something brand new. She asks me what I'm doing in Berlin, I tell her I'm stopping here on the way to see a friend, I'm a writer and I'm hoping to write about my friend and my trip and everything and she asks, "Will you write about me?" and I say, "If you want me to I could, yes," and she says, "I'd like that." And it's nice to sit next to her and in the moment when we're alone she asks me for my number and she says, "I mean, you probably have lots of free time, can I show you around a little?"

The next day I get two messages, one from Nico that reads:

hey! how's Berlin so far?

and another from Jana that reads:

hey, nice to meet you. Let's get a coffee today, ja?

and I write to Nico:

it's good. where should I meet you when I get to Rome?

I meet with Jana for coffee too. We meet for a coffee in the late afternoon and we talk and she tells me about growing up in Berlin, the first generation after the wall came down, the raves in the nineties, "I was still a kid," she says, "sneaking around with these junkies, it was wild. Everything was different after the wall came down, everything changed and we acted like it was normal right away, there wasn't a moment to think," and I tell her some things but I don't tell her the heavy things, there's no Nico, there's no heart attack, it's all lightness, it's all laughter and hair. She brings me to the top of the Berliner Dom as the sun begins to set and we watch the city turn dark from there, from above everything, and she points to a building in the distance and she says, "That's where Damiel tried to save the man who jumped." I don't know what she means.

It's night and I bring Jana to show her my favourite thing I've seen so far in Berlin. We walk down a dark street and there's a statue twelve feet tall at least of a great green-and-blue frog king, it's reaching out its hand, its hand outstretched, a heavy crown on its ugly psychedelic head lit bright by a street light, the neon light of the bar nearby, its paint

146

coming off in patches from age and from weather and the hands reaching toward it in the long exposed night, its eyes bright and dulling. Jana laughs and says, "It's just a statue outside a bar!" and I say I know but look at it and I think she'll kiss me now but she doesn't and it's okay because she laughs and she touches my arm. She says, "I'll show you my favourite thing. Meine Lieblingssache. Tomorrow we'll go to the Berlin State Library. It's where Damiel and Cassiel meet in *Wings of Desire*," and I laugh because the things she says make me laugh and I don't understand and I say I don't know what that means and she says, "You know, Wim Wenders? *Wings of Desire?*" and I don't know.

Jana brings me to her home, a two-bedroom flat in Neu-kölln. It's on the main floor, the front windows almost an extension of the sidewalk, no curtains. She sits me on her faded yellow couch and we watch the movie *Wings of Desire* so far apart at first like teenagers, near the end we're sitting next to each other our legs touching, our hands touching, our bodies being pulled into each other. The people walking past in the street outside, right next to us, are looking into us, everybody watching now like they're part of all of this too, all of us together. She doesn't kiss me, we won't kiss and we fall asleep there together and I wake up and she's gone and it's morning and I'm alone in this apartment now.

I get on my shoes and go. I'm in the street now, walking away, and I get a message from Nico:

meet me tomorrow at Termini. keep an eye on your stuff. not to scare you but if you get robbed in Rome it'll definitely happen at Termini :)

I think maybe I shouldn't go. Maybe I should stay here where I met this woman. I wonder if I should go back to her now. But no, I came for something else.

I message Nico back and I say:

okay. I'm on my way to the bus now. it'll be a long trip to you, wish me luck.

II

The second time I saw Nico was by accident. I go to a show at Massey Hall and the opener is a local band I've never heard of and they're good, someone tells me, so I go early and the cream-coloured curtain rises to the rafters and there she is, Nico, on the stage, sitting at the rear of the stage at a piano behind a lot of men with guitars and a lot of women singing, playing drums. I sit watching her every move. Not once does she look out at the audience, not once does she look in my direction. I don't want her to go. Stay there, play piano all night. When it's over she walks off the stage without a look not even a wave and the main act comes on and I sit reluctant now waiting for the show to end to find her and I wait outside at the artist entrance staring at the door like a dog waiting to come inside until she comes out and she sees me and stops.

"Hey," she says. "What are you doing here?"

"Hey, sorry, um, I didn't know you were playing, I saw you play it was really good, I thought I'd wait and say hi. I wanted to see you and say hi."

"This isn't the best time. Um," she says, looking back at the door she'd just come out of. "Let's meet tomorrow?"

"Where?"

She says, I don't know, meet me at the house we laid on top of, that night that we met, she says, "I have to go," and she stays. She stays and she touches me on the arm and I say, "Okay," and she stays and she stays and another moment still she stays and she goes back inside.

The next day I wait in front of the house and I wait and I think she's not coming, she has to come. She might already be on the roof, I climb up the fire escape think maybe she's here, she has to be here and there she is, facing away, sitting where we laid together once, that one time, like she hasn't moved since that time but something gone now what feels now like long ago.

"Hi," she says.

"Hey. Nice to see you."

"Yeah, same. I'm glad you came."

"Of course. Sorry to surprise you like that last night, maybe I should have just left."

"No, I'm glad you came after me finally."

"How have you been?"

"Well, not great I guess. I thought about you," she says. There's a sound in the distance like a low hum, streaks of cloud in the sky. "I don't have much time. I wanted to tell you something. I should have told you before. I could have called you. I didn't know if I could," she says, and she tells me that after we met, soon after, she'd checked herself into the psych ward at the hospital. She didn't speak for two weeks, the entire time she was there. Something was wrong with her and she didn't know what it was and she needed to face it. "It had nothing to do with you. You jumped into my life at a bad moment."

Oh, I say. Are you okay? I'm better. Do you want to talk about it? Not really. What do you want to talk about? Nothing. Let's just sit.

We sit there silent. She puts her head on my shoulder. I think she's asleep and she says, "You should know too, I liked you. I wanted to see you again. But you were sweet and I thought: I'll hurt this one. I'll run away and I'll hurt him and then I'll hurt too. And I'm married now. I got married. I think I still like you. Do you feel that? I know it was only one night but it felt real, it felt like a lifetime, didn't it?

When I got out of the hospital I met someone. His name is Robert and he's really nice to me. He's patient and he treats me better than anyone has ever treated me. We got married a couple months ago. I'm sorry."

"Oh," I say. "You're here now though."

"I am."

"So. Okay. Can we do this again another time?"

"Of course."

"Then okay," I say.

"You're not upset?"

"You're happy, right?"

"Yeah, I am. I love Robert, he's always there for me."

"Then great," I say. We talk some more and we're quiet some more and I ask do you still live here? and she says where? and I say in this building and she says, "What? I don't live here, no." I ask who does? and she says, "I don't know, who cares?" and we watch the sun go down, all of the strangers below us living their lives, all of us together. I meet Robert a few months later, Nico coming into my life every few months, every few years, not so much anymore and Robert kisses me on both cheeks because he's Italian too and it's nice, a heat like Italian kindness and it's nice to have a friend who you love, who you want to be married to, who you'd marry their husband too if she asked, all of us married together someday maybe.

II

The bus brings me to Munich where I get on another bus that brings me to Florence where I get on a train to Rome, so many hours of moving, the country passing by me in darkness and in sleep. When the sun is out the morning Italian countryside opens from the window of the train like the curtains of a stage play. So much ruin, stone buildings, broken houses, dead autumn trees, muddy ground, brown muddy water. I'm going 242 km/h through the middle of a mountain and the man across from me is listening to an audio book, I can hear it, something pulp, something beautiful and it's golden and I breathe differently here, the sunlight sharp, crystalline.

No one robs me at Termini. Nico is there waiting. She looks different from the last time I saw her, her round and full moon face has sharpened, she's stronger and composed of the same stuff a star is composed of, not the star in the sky but the star on the movie screen legs crossed and cool, so cool. "How are you, darling?" she says as she takes off her sunglasses so large they hide her face and she kisses my cheek, we take the subway to her home next to the great pyramid overlooking the Protestant Cemetery.

"I almost died," she says, as she prepares a plate of bread and tomatoes, cheese and prosciutto. "Would you like Merlot or Montepulciano?"

She lights a cigarette at the window and we see her neighbour, an old woman across the street, changing her clothes and she's naked in front of us and neither of us mentions it. Nico says, "Italy is so strange, everything happens in the open. You might not see it the same way. I think you see things differently than I do. To me everything is beautiful like it's made of gold and garlanded. It's like a soap opera brothel." She tells me about her job teaching English to Italian teenagers, how they hit on her every day, "It's really charming," she says, a long drag of her long cigarette, and she brings up her heart attack. I take out my audio recorder and I ask, "Do you mind if I record this conversation?" and she says, "Yeah, that's fine. What for?" and I say I don't know, I just feel it's important to take down, maybe I'll write something about all this someday if you're okay with that and she says, "Yeah, that would be fine I suppose."

There's a click and a shuffling, a little silence.

"Okay, it's on."

"Okay."

"So what happened. You had a heart attack?"

"Kind of. I oversimplified it for a lot of people because it's easier that way. It's something people can understand. What happened is I had several massive blood clots and my lung collapsed. I had what's called a pulmonary embolism. I was in some real danger for a time. I had to be hooked up to a breathing machine."

"But wait, go back a little. When did this happen?"

"It was in the winter. I remember because we'd just signed the lease on our house and had just moved in. Poor Robert had to paint all the inside of the house by himself because I was laid out in a sickbed. You remember Robert, my husband?"

"Yeah. How is he?"

"He's fine. He doesn't like that I'm here but we're still married. We still love each other of course. I miss him. He's very patient with me. But sorry, what happened is I started experiencing a little bit of pain in my leg as if it was the only part of my body that I'd worked out. Also later here in my chest. It was very mild. I almost didn't think much of it but I happened to mention it to the pharmacist when... what I had done... I'll be honest. Don't use this if you write something about this okay?"

"Of course."

"Well, I'd gone to the pharmacy to dispose of a set of pills that I'd been stockpiling in the event of a suicide attempt.

I was like, I've got my shit together. I've got to be serious about this living thing. But I'm struggling with those ideas again now. I feel like it should be simpler because I've been given this new lease on life and I feel like I have the responsibility to make the most of it but... Do you want some more wine?"

"Sure, yeah. Thank you."

"So I disposed of those pills. While I was there I said to the pharmacist, 'Hey, I'm experiencing this pain in my chest and had a little bit in my leg, did I do something?' She took my blood pressure and she suggested that I go to the emergency room. It was initially misdiagnosed as a musculoskeletal problem but later that night I experienced difficulty walking and sleeping and breathing and it was as though this whole side of my body had shut down. Robert took me to emergency in the morning. He stayed up all night, I wouldn't leave the house. I wouldn't let him take me anywhere. I was being so stubborn. It wasn't until he had to go to work and I realized I'd be in this big house where I felt so alone without him, like an intruder. It was then that I let him drive me there."

"Ha! Good for him."

"Yeah. Well, I ended up in hospital for twelve days. At first I had a quite serious breathing regimen. I had a giant oxygen bypass machine because one of my lungs wasn't willing to behave like a lung. Then slowly I was put on less and less oxygen as my lung came back to itself. I started to breathe normally but I still thought I was going to die."

"How do you feel now?"

"Well...you go through something like that and it knocks you for a loop. I sort of have... I feel shame... Sometimes I brush up against existential angst. Lately there's been a whole shit ton of that. And I feel guilty that my will to live was shaken by this sort of physical, medical catastrophe because if I'm serious about my shit it ought to be unshakable. But it shook me hard..."

"We don't have to talk about it if you don't want to."

"No, I want to. This is good, keep asking me questions."

"Okay, what was it like being in the hospital?"

"Oh it was so repetitious. Any time a doctor came to see me was like a jolt of anticipation. Like, what are they going to tell me now? Am I going to learn something that's going to get me out of here quicker? I also had so many visitors, which was so kind of people. You learn that people care. That's one of the reasons I'm trying hard not to give up now. There's a part of me that wants to start stockpiling medication again. Also I'm now on blood thinners for the rest of my life. If I take too many of those I'd start bleeding internally and then I'd really be in for it. I would have to face the consequences of that action. There's definitely part of me that wants to do something drastic because I don't know what I'm doing with my life now and I don't know what I want to be doing and I've been sliding into despair. Like, what am I doing? Why did I leave my husband and everything I knew to come here?"

"I guess that's something you'll figure out eventually."

"Yeah…I know how many people I would be letting down to go down that path without being prompted. The pulmonary embolism was something I didn't choose. Choosing to kill myself would be a betrayal of these people who love me. Whether it makes ultimate sense or not, whether I've lived a life that merits that kind of goodwill, I feel like I have the responsibility to honour people's love. Especially if I'm going to be at all consistent in my view regarding the primacy of love in general because I really do want to live that way. Like, I promised someone I'd be around. I have to be around for him."

We should go to dinner, she says, I'll show you how the Romans live.

Rome is warm and there are ruins everywhere, Nico walks me through her street, through the courtyards, couples kissing, couples eating gelato old men in sweat-stained suits. We walk into a wine store and there are tables inside, people eating entire meals, dogs sitting under their tables, all of them yelling *sì sì! grazie!* and I hear Nico on the other side of the store and she's yelling in Italian at an old man behind a counter who is eating a breadstick big as a finger on his hand, his hand like a loaf of bread, and I stand behind her and she gives him money and we leave and I ask her are you okay? What was that? She says, "What?" I say you were yelling at that guy and she says, "Oh we were just talking." We walk along a river. The sun is going down now, we're at the Colisseum and she opens our bottle of wine and she passes it to me and she says, "This is a touristy thing. Whatever, it's neat right? People used to watch other people die here every day. It was entertainment."

We go to a bar and Nico orders us drinks and there's a great feast in the room like a buffet all couscous, bread, pasta, and salads. We eat and we drink and when she's in the bathroom I notice a man at the table across from us and he says, "I heard you speaking English."

"I was, yes."

"Where are you from?"

I hesitate, I think of what Nico told me about Termini, to be careful here. To keep up my guard. I tell him North America.

"Nice," he says, and he stares at me and a moment passes and I ask where he's from. "I'm from Colombia," he says, "I'm a magician, can I show you a magic trick?"

"No, thank you."

"What about your friend, can I ask her?"

"You can ask her if you like, I don't think she'll be into it either."

When Nico comes back the man asks her, "Do you want to see a magic trick?" and she says, "Oh my god, yes! Of course!" and her eyes light up. The Colombian shows us his trick and then he asks for money and we both say no, sorry, and he goes back to his table and he doesn't look at us and later Nico says, "I liked his trick, didn't you?" I laugh and I say no, I don't need card tricks and she says, "I never knew you weren't fun," the reflection of the moon in her hair, a woman somewhere nearby singing what sounds like "Wild Horses" by the Rolling Stones, a song from another place entirely, another era, in a thick, luxurious Italian accent like a hand gliding against the grain of a velvet bedsheet. Then I'm asleep on her couch and I dream of Nico still, we're still walking through Rome in the night but then she changes and she's Jana now and she holds a bullfrog in the small palm of her small hand and says *look* and I look into its eyes, the eyes of the frog like human eyes like the eyes of her and I'm startled awake and it's the dim part of the pre-morning and Nico is moving silent through the room, she's here and she turns to me and I'm awake and she's smiling at me, good morning, something calm washes over, all the colours of the world inside of me I'll never forget it. She says she has to leave.

I walk through Rome. I walk to the museum of John Keats,

I read the letters of John Keats, I stand in the room where John Keats died, I stare into his death mask faded yellow. Outside tourists line the Spanish Steps, the entire Piazza photographed twenty times per second where once it was empty, once a man wrote here and this is where he died. I eat pizza, I drink wine, everywhere people yelling and laughing *sì! sì! buono grazie!* When Nico finds me in her home I'm reading Keats's "Ode to a Grecian Urn" and she tells me she can't stay, she has to go back to work. We drink a glass of wine and she tells me about her day and it's like laying your heavy naked body in the flowing Trevi Fountain just hearing her speak. She leaves and I get a message from Jana that says:

hey! where did you go? I just went out to get some coffee for us and you were gone

and another one that reads:

sorry you left, I hope you're okay. Let's hang out again soon?

and they're dated from three days ago. I write her back and I say:

hey, sorry I'm in Rome. my phone has been dead. I might come back in a couple days, will you be there? I'd like to see you again

II

The next day is my last day in Rome. I'm restless. Nico is

at work and I'm in her apartment and it's raining outside and I'm reading and I'm on my computer and I want to be moving, I'm stuck. When Nico gets home she has to leave again for a dinner with her boss, "It's a gala," she says, "I'm sorry I haven't had much time for you," she says and it's okay, I say, you're alive and that's what I wanted and she changes into a long black dress and she's more beautiful than I've ever seen her, she's the most beautiful woman I've ever seen, or maybe it's more that something lingers from when someone else loved me and it withers inside, the erosion of stone from simple time, and anyway Nico and I are here, my time with Nico, not all these moments that come are gone too fast I suppose. She asks me, "How do I look?" and I say, "You look great," and I want to say you're the most beautiful woman in the world and I want to mean it and I hesitate, it's the best I can do with Robert back at home, lovely Robert so lovely he never hurt me either and I love him too. I say, "Hey, I haven't heard you play piano this whole time I've been here," and she says yeah, I don't do that anymore, I'm a different person now, different from before and, "Anyway," she says, "by the way, I promised you I'd stick around too." She leaves and I book a ticket back to Berlin and in the morning I say goodbye to Nico.

I say goodbye to Nico and I fly back to Berlin.

II

I get a message from Jana when I get to Berlin, it says:

I brought Amir to Munich for the next few days, we're visiting friends. come to Munich. Come see me

and I'm out of money and I'm almost out of credit and I'll make it back to Canada with a few dollars left. I can't go to Munich. I won't see Jana again.

I have a few days left and I meet a woman in a café and she talks to me and she talks a lot about herself but I don't mind, I'm alone in a place that might as well be the middle of the ocean so far away from land. She asks me if I want to go to a dinner party and I say yes. She brings me to some Turkish markets and she speaks to the vendors in Turkish and they laugh and it's so charming and she takes me by the arm and it's like we're a couple now, we're walking arm in arm our steps matching perfect as we walk through Kreuzberg our hands full of food and we get to her friend's apartment through the dark halls, the lights don't work, the switches don't turn and we find their apartment giggling in the dark and they welcome us hello. And it's nice, they're kind, they welcome me and we speak, I act like the charming guest asking questions, where are you from, what do you do, this is a beautiful wine, isn't it? A woman comes in late and she sits next to me at the great meal we're all sharing and she's drunk and she looks at me, up and down, and not looking at me now she asks everyone else, "Who's this guy?" and no one answers her and I say hello as she turns her head and talks to someone else. They all get drunker and they all speak in Turkish and I can't understand what's being said, I haven't said anything in a long time and the woman

I came with isn't here now, where is she? What was her name again? I can't remember now. The woman next to me asks, "Why are you so quiet?" and she laughs and she pours wine for everyone but me. A man who was kind to me earlier in the night looks at me and says something serious in Turkish and everyone is quiet now and every face is aimed at me. Someone asks, "Are you okay? Are we making you uncomfortable?" I say no, I'm happy to have been invited and the woman next to me laughs and she says, "What are you doing here anyway? Tell us something: Who are you? What do you do?" I say I was invited here, I'm from Toronto, I'm a writer, I'm writing about the things I do here to remember them better and she says, "So what, you're going to go home, you're going to write a story about a terrible woman you met at a terrible dinner party or something? And no one wanted you there? There's something to write about, there's something for you to remember," and I say no, it's not like that, it's not a weapon. The silence of the room is loud now like the engine of a plane. I get up from my seat and I put on my shoes and my coat, the people in the kitchen laughing, I can't find my bag, the woman I came with she must have taken it, she must have left with my bag, my clothes and devices, the book I'd been writing in and my recorder with all of Nico's words, every memory of her and of here gone. I leave, my legs brushing together through the silence of the dark hallways down to the street.

I walk through Berlin, the wide streets and the döner shops and the Berlin Victory Column looking down on me somewhere near and the so many languages everywhere I don't understand and I go back to the bar with the dog, with Georgie. The bartender says, "Hey, nice to see you again!" and I don't see Georgie anywhere and I ask, "Hey, where's Georgie?"

"Ah, he's run off," the bartender says. Oh no, I say, what happened? "He does this from time to time, he's fine I'd bet. Little bird, that one, free as," he says and he looks out the window like maybe he's outside right now, maybe that's him, and his eyes are searching. Georgie is gone.

The next day I go back to Toronto.

The Sword

I'M DRIVING NORTH AROUND THE GREAT LAKES AND LAKE
Simcoe and Perry Sound, past a place called Moon River
and a place called Swords, past Horseshoe Lake and Killbear
Park and Still River, the Lost Channel, I'm driving to the
French River where Matt lives, him and his wife, Nancy, a
woman he met and he left with and they disappeared together a few years ago, no goodbyes to anyone just gone,
haven't seen him since. It's winter and it's dark and the heat
doesn't work in this car that I rented because you can't get
to him any other way than by car and because you continue
in life, no matter what, you owe that to someone, anyone,
everyone. So I'm wrapped up in all the clothes I brought,
two shirts, a sweater and a coat, a Mexican blanket, a black
scarf with red roses wrapped around my face.

The last time I saw Matt he drove me and Rienne to a lake
just outside Toronto, where we all lived then, the three of
us, and Rienne and Matt had been together for a while,
longer than I knew any two people to be together, they
were in love I thought and I remember a great mist that day
and we came to a bridge rusted red and brown and it was
blocked off, signs saying *Danger, Bridge Out of Order*, and we

walk to the middle of the bridge and we're laughing like we could die, don't die, and an old man comes down the path on the other end of the bridge and he walks over to us and he says, "Y'all fishin?"

"Nah, man," Matt says to him. "You?"

"Not today," he says, "not ever. I done enough fishin for my life," and he says y'all have a good day and Matt says, "You too, careful on the bridge, yeah?" and the man says mmm hmm and keeps walking past.

"You know that guy?" I ask Matt.

"Nah, I've seen him here before though. I came out last week and he was here fishing."

"I didn't know you've been out here before," Rienne says and Matt says mmm hmm.

Matt brings a piece of wood and some rope out onto the bridge, a handful of screws and nuts and a wrench and a screwdriver, a lighter, and he sits on the bridge building a swing and I swim in the water under the bridge with Rienne, the water cold and brown and Rienne says, "Is that a fish?" and I say no, no way, there's no fish here and then Matt lowers the swing down to the water and he ties it to the bridge and he yells out, "Okay, try it out!"

"Is it safe?" I yell back up to him and he laughs like a hyena laughs and yells back, "Just do it!" so I pull myself up onto the wooden seat and the rope tightens but it doesn't break and I swing back and forth, slowly, being careful in my movement, my eyes up to the bridge watching, waiting for something to break but nothing, my feet dangling above the cold water, and we swing back and forth, the three of us, toward and away from each other and away and back and forth between the red rusted bridge and the cold and fishless brown water and we leave the swing there for someone else to use up when we all go and I don't hear from Matt after that for a long time. Rienne goes home and she doesn't say goodbye when she leaves the car, Matt and I go to the Rainbow Bar that night and I see him talking to a woman and then he's gone. People will tell me they saw him around the city a few times that week, every time with that woman, and then I hear they drove down to the Grand Canyon together and then I don't hear anything else for a while. Sometimes I'd be out and I'd hear a laugh like his and it was never him and that was hard. Then Rienne leaves and she moves out west because it's all too hard for her. She didn't deal well with losing him. It was a difficult time and we weren't ready for it, we all keep moving like pieces in a Rube Goldberg machine. Just me now.

When I get to Matt's trailer I knock on the door, puffed up with clothes like a hot marshmallow, I imagine him opening the door and that laughter but no one answers and I knock again and nothing. I look through the window and there he is, Matt, sleeping on the couch in his underwear the TV on, the TV glow makes neon his near-naked body. I knock on the window and he doesn't move, still dreaming there alone. I go to my car and I sit in it and I sound the horn over and over, one loud blast of cold sent out after another, cold horn blast over and over, into the dark and cold winter forest, over the frozen lake and only I can hear it. I think about Rienne and I consider calling her because I miss her too but she's so far away now. I spoke to her a few days before, a few hours after Matt sent me a message saying,

hey, yer boy is a Papa now

and I said

lol what?

and then he told me, the marriage, the baby, everything, he said,

come visit, come see her.

I called Rienne soon after that, she said, "Hey! So nice to hear from you, what's up?"

"Nothing, I just thought of you, wanted to check in and see how you're doing."

"That's sweet, I'm doing okay. I'm walking home right now. I might go to yoga but I don't know, it's been a long day and I'd love to lie down instead."

"Yoga is kind of like lying down."

"Not the kind I do, bud. Hot yoga. It gets pretty sweaty in there, it's like a whole body workout. You sweat everything out, everything that's good and bad inside of you, you just leave it as a pool of water on the floor. It's really freeing, you just let everything go and then you're fresh, you can be whoever you want to be after that."

"Who do you want to be?"

"Well, I met this woman the other day, she's part of this scooter club where her and her friends rent scooters and drive around the city together. She invited me to do that later, it's kind of dorky but I don't know, I might want to be that right now. Plus I'm pretty sure she's into me and she's hot. I haven't been on a date in a while so maybe it's time I be dorky scooter me."

"Oh, I thought you were dating someone."

"You mean Alex? We broke up about a week ago."

"Oh wow, I'm sorry, are you okay?"

"Yeah, I mean it wasn't fun but it was for the best. He just wanted a lot more than I wanted. He's getting to a point where his friends are getting married and having a wife and kid are really important to him. I just wasn't into it. Not with him anyway. I love him, I love his guts but I just didn't see doing that with him."

"Do you ever see doing that?"

"Yeah, of course. I mean, I thought I'd do that with Matt but since then I've just gone in a whole other direction. Like, maybe I could do that with someone else but if I never do I won't die, I'll just keep doing whatever I want to do whenever I want to do it," and she laughs and she sounds a little defeated and a lot happy too and I ask her do you ever talk to him? Matt? and she says, "No. I've thought about it. Maybe someday. I'll wait until the time is right," and we talk a little more and I don't tell her about Matt, that he has a family now with someone else, because it's hard to tell someone that the thing in their heart so fearsome they can't even breathe it has found the sharp breath of life and it's winged and it's a beautiful thing that the rest of us will celebrate. And I'm outside Matt's trailer, in the winter, in the dark, in the snow, my toes are losing their feeling and I get a rock, ready to break Matt's window and he opens the door half sleeping.

"Hey!" he yells. "Quit fucking making noise and come inside, Jesus it's cold!" and he dances there in the doorway in the cold as I go to him.

"What are you doing in all those clothes!" he says, in his underwear. "Give me some of them!" I take off layer after layer of coat, sweater, shirt, and I throw them all at him in this warm trailer, burning wood fire makes the air warm and dry and he puts on my sweater and he puts on my jacket and we laugh and he says, "Oh man, that's better, it was so cold in here. You want a drink or something? Come in, bud."

We sit at the dining room table which is an arm's length from the kitchen and a step away from everything else in his small home and we drink whisky, what little he has left from his wedding, he says, "Nancy's dad gave me this big bottle of good whisky I guess, I don't know, it's okay," and he laughs and his laugh is different now, deeper, more guttural, still animal but different.

"Where is Nancy? I'm excited to meet her."

"Oh she went to her dad's place for the night."

"Everything okay?"

"Yeah, her dad gets lonesome sometimes because her mom died a couple years ago so she likes to visit a couple nights a week."

"What happened to her?"

"Her mom? She killed herself."

"Oh wow. Sorry to hear it."

"Yeah. It happened like right before I met Nancy actually. She was kind of a mess about it so I was just there, you know? And my dad had died and I was kind of fucked up too. Anyway her dad is awesome, he's a welder. He makes swords! He gave me this awesome sword at our wedding!" and he pulls out a great broadsword, long as a man is long, and he swings it around and says, "I've been practising with it. I can cut a fuckin pumpkin in half."

"Careful, you got a kid, better keep it away from her."

"Oh yeah!" he says and he runs three steps to the TV almost falling over, almost falling onto the sword, and he pulls a picture frame and throws it to me like a frisbee I fumble with and when it's in my hand I look and there's a photo of him and the woman I saw him with at the Rainbow Bar, older now, his wife, Nancy, and he's holding a baby too.

"Her name is Juniper Loup."

"Wow, congratulations. What a great name. How old is she?"

"Just a couple months. Nancy wasn't hot on the name at first, it took some convincing. Do you remember? It was where we stayed at the Grand Canyon, when you and me went there a few years ago."

"Oh whoa, right, I remember yeah," we sit at his kitchen table in his home, the home he owns with his wife and child, full of love, far away from the Grand Canyon, him wearing my clothes. He asks if I want to watch a movie or something. I say yeah, whatever, man, I'm your guest and he says, "I have some MDMA too, we could do that if you want," and I laugh and I say don't you have a kid? and he says, "Well, the kid ain't here."

We each take a little bit and we watch a movie and the movie is about a man who falls in love with a woman, he and his friend and the woman move into a house together and then the woman falls in love with the friend. It's hard but they work it out, they all stay together and the relationships change and then she falls back in love with the first man and I wonder if the two men will fall in love too and we're both pretty quiet through it and it's warm and my breathing is changing slowly, slowly I go from light nervous breathing to normal then deep breaths, every few minutes, my heart moving to the front of my chest, sighing and yawning. Now Matt is laughing and I'm laughing and he says, "Oh man, I can't do this, this movie is so bad. Let's go outside, I gotta show you something."

We dress up real warm, warm sweaters, warm coats, already sweating and Matt looks terrifying and beautiful as he moves through the night like a scarecrow with his sword under the moon under the mountain, him swaying back and forth like the gentle roses in the flesh-coloured vases of the bars we used to roam and he brings me walking down a path through the woods behind his trailer, still dark, and he leads me to what looks like a great, long, and winding flat field of snow but no it's a frozen body of water, the river I suppose, and we watch together, watching down the river into the clear open horizon framed by two forests, frozen river, and sky as the full moon looks back at us like a huge blue mirror. We lie down in the snow, the silence of the forest everywhere and dark, just our hearts and then there's a howl in the distance and Matt laughs and he says, "I think that's just a dog."

"It's not even cold out here."

"I know, it's fucked, I'm still sweating."

"We could sleep here, I bet."

"Yeah, but I got a kid."

"That must be crazy."

"Not really," he says. "Like it just happened. Nancy was pregnant and she wanted to keep it and I said alright, let's make a go of this, so we did. And then it just happened."

"What was the birth like?"

"Oh man, *that* was crazy. Like we planned out everything, we did it at home in our bed, Nancy had been working with a doula for a few months, she was ready. Then it happened and it was like there was blood everywhere and all this stuff, it was like Nancy wasn't there, she would scream like fully scream and then her eyes would roll into the back of her head and she would go completely silent, it was so intense. Then she'd start screaming again. It was like a witch's ritual, like it was really dark and out of control. And she doesn't remember anything! It's fucked. Like we thought we were ready but then when it happened it was like we definitely weren't ready for that."

"What was it like seeing Juniper for the first time?"

"I don't know, man. Like I didn't see any point in having anyone else in my life anymore, I really let go of everything once I saw that kid. Oh man."

"Do you ever talk to Rienne?" I ask him and I wasn't sure I'd ask him this because it's difficult to ask someone to access a part of themselves that might be deeply painful but we're high and something like love is flowing through me and I think okay, it's okay to do this.

"Not really," he says, "I sent her a message and apologized for disappearing like I did but she never wrote me back. I get it though. I hurt her bad. I think it would hurt both of us if I kept trying to contact her, you know? Like when she's ready she'll come to me. I miss her a lot, I think about her all the time," and then he says, "When my dad died I freaked out a little bit and she didn't get it. She became really cold to me, like really distant, she just didn't understand why I was acting the way I was acting. It was like my entire past was erased, like everyone passes in and out of my life but my dad was always there, he knew me in every part of my life and now he was gone. I felt like a big part of me went with him. Rienne could only see this imaginary future we were going to share, she didn't get it, she wasn't there for me. I don't blame her. But I met Nancy and her mom had just passed, I understood her and she understood me and that was it, I just went for it."

I think about the pain I saw Rienne go through when Matt disappeared. I think, she knows now, she knows loss now. And also I get it, it's okay. We're all okay.

"Yeah, man," he says. "Do you think you'll have kids?"

"There was a point where I would have had kids," I say, "but that moment's gone." I know loss now too.

We hear the howl again and we get up and we walk and Matt says, "I got this sword, we'll be alright," and when we get back to his trailer we take off all our warm clothes and we race out into the backyard in our underwear and we roll in the snow and it sticks to the adrenaline sweat of our bodies and we go back inside and we sit next to each other at the stove, our bodies touching, laughing like hyenas.

Late the next morning we're drinking coffee at the table and Nancy is home with the baby, Juniper, and Matt takes Juni in his arms, cradles her there between his arm and chest and he's shirtless now at the stove frying bacon dancing like he used to dance, dancing like a stripper, him and this child, him making faces making the child laugh, his wife laughing too and I think back to once when I knew Matt and he was with Rienne then and we were all drinking and it was late like it always was then and they were making this great, grand painting on this great, large canvas and they were making it together and Matt held Rienne, his arm around her shoulder, pulled her close and he seemed happier than he'd ever been then and he said, "Let's have a baby together! All three of us! Do you wanna?" and Rienne laughed and she looked at him the way this baby was looking at him now. And all of that is gone now I suppose, these three laughing and dancing together with the ghost of that great painting under the moon, under the mountain.

Nancy, who is so kind to me and calm, she asks if I want to hold Juni and I say, "Sure." She puts her child in my arms without teaching me how, just gives her to me and I'm not ready and she says, "She'll trust you if you trust yourself," and I'm holding her and I'm swinging with her and I'm ready and I'm letting go of something, looking at this baby thinking I could love you, I could love someone, I could let someone love me, okay I will.

The Australian

I GET A JOB AT THE RAINBOW BAR, I GO IN FOUR SOMETIMES five nights sometimes six nights a week, bartending, having fun, escaping. Friends come in and I give them free drinks and sometimes strange women flirt with me, sometimes strange men too, it's nice, I never have to go anywhere to find love this is it, it's always free shots and a kiss from a friend and a kiss from a stranger and a candle or anything on fire in front of me, every night is warm lights and candles and I don't long for a single thing. And it is this way for a little while. In time, while the candles are still burning, mid-shot, the room gets a little smaller and the air gets a little darker and my friends move away or they stop coming in and sometimes it's so slow that time stops and all the regulars who want to forget, they look at me with suspicion and they're there now to be drunk and to forget and I'm there to take their money. Maybe the only difference between us in time is the exchange of money, I'm saving money for months on end, I have more money than I know what to do with and not much else, no daylight, all the faces of night blur into the morning the sounds of their voices still ringing through my bones. The people who are my friends now, the people I work with, go home to their partners and they drink so they fight a lot. As much laughter as I hear and tenderness that I see I also see crying, drinking, cocaine, no sleep, sober again wrapped in blankets and again and I go home my pockets full of money, an empty apartment. This kind of living, how long do I work there? How many months is this month? How many days?

One night Petra, a woman I work with more than anyone else, often every night, she comes in to work crying and she tells me that her boyfriend cheated on her and she's shaking and she apologizes for crying and I tell her it's okay, she doesn't have to be here if she doesn't want to be, I'm fine working alone and her friend comes, a woman I only ever see with Petra when they're drinking and her friend is sad too and they sit at a table weeping, both of them, both of them drunk both of them crying and I don't envy Petra now and the night gets so busy I'm overwhelmed and everything happens at once like a snap of the fingers of a rude customer trying to get my attention leaning over the bar and yelling, I go home with more money than I've ever made in a night and I look in the mirror and the person looking back at me is thinner than I remembered, another person entirely, eyes sunken still bright. I haven't written anything in months.

II

It's winter and it's morning and I'm microdosing, careful not to take more than I can handle, to not be overwhelmed, and I meet with Sally and Ed to eat breakfast together in a restaurant close to the Rainbow Bar because it's always there somewhere in the background and we sit together my body light, sometimes too light like I could fly away but no it's not enough for that, it's enough to float, a ship in the Pacific dipping up and down, a plane in turbulence. We haven't known each other long at this point, Sally and Ed and I, I met them through some friends a few months back, in the dog days of summer where every day was the same and beautiful, hot and lazy days of drinking and they were lovely together, they welcomed me in, whoever they met, and made me feel part of their world and I ask them, "How did you two meet anyway?"

"It was a while back," Sally tells me, "two years ago, I think?"

"Three," Ed says.

"Are you sure?"

"Yeah, it was the same year we drove down to Detroit and the election was happening."

"Oh yeah, remember that bar we went to and we watched the Obama and Romney debate?"

Ed laughs, "Yeah, that was crazy."

"So it was three years ago. I was living in a commune. I didn't realize it was a commune at first, I thought it was just some buds living in a house together but it was like up at dawn, gardening, house meetings, communal meals, lots of planning. I was a kid, I thought that was just how adults lived. Not that they were kids, I was the youngest one there, I think. But we built this stage in this old big black barn out back and we'd invite bands to come play once a month. Oh man, we'd have these huge parties with all the locals. It turned out to be a good way to get in good with the community. Lots of old folx. Weird old-timers. We'd all get dressed up in dresses or in drag, it was a blast. But because the house was in the middle of nowhere I'd have to drive into town and pick up the bands in this big Cadillac. I'd drive them through the country, real slow along the dirt roads because they were hell on the engine undertray. I remember the car was all wood panelled and painted blue, oh man I loved that car.

"So one time I picked up this band and they had this manic, laughing energy and they all came giggling into the car laughing and a mess. Shit, if it wasn't intoxicating. I loved these guys right away. But you know, it was also really overwhelming too. Like so much that I thought I'd have a panic attack. Then I noticed the boy in the back seat not laughing. He was more thoughtful. He was looking out the window looking sad, watching birds circling above us in the sky. Something inside me said I'd fall in love with that boy right then."

Later, when Sally is in the bathroom, just Ed and me now, Ed says, like it's a secret, "You know, it's funny. Sally loves telling that story. To be honest I don't remember a lot of that stuff. Like, for me it wasn't fireworks right away. I don't even remember that car ride. I do remember meeting her that night though. She was so insistent that we dance together, she wasn't taking no for an answer. Not that I wanted to say no, she was cute. I remember she was dressed in a blue suit with a beard of blue glitter. I remember she held my hand and led me through that party and it was sweet. I remember being charmed. But I thought it would only be that night. It was a while after that, after she called me a bunch and we started writing letters and then she moved to Toronto and we dated for about a month or two and blah blah blah, before I think I started feeling what she felt. It was something. But I was really aloof for a long time." And then he says something like it's funny, these stories you share are always different depending on who tells them and when they're told, right?

By then we're finished eating and the light coming through the window is becoming too much for me and I say, "I might have to go home," even though we made plans to spend the day together but I leave because it's right for me right now and I go home and I lie alone on my couch watching the sky through the window, the simple clouds rolling and folding into themselves, opening and closing like a curtain, something wonderful for only myself now.

Later I'm feeling more grounded and I go back out to find Sally and Ed again but they're gone, not answering their phones, not at home, the night coming on and the cool night air and a co-worker calls wanting me to fill in at work because he's in a fight with his partner and doesn't want to leave, I say okay, I'll be there soon, I'm wearing a golden yellow sweater, frayed and too hot for working but I have to because it's all I have and I only mention the sweater because at work, sweating, the lilt of coming down floating through my body, the wonderful feeling of the afternoon lingering, this woman comes up to me and she motions with her finger for me to come closer because everything is loud, her mouth grazing my ear she says, "I like your jumper," but with an Australian accent, the sound of it confused like, "Ah liek yah jumpah," and I laugh and I say, "Excuse me?" and she looks at me the same way I'd been looking at those clouds earlier that day, the music in the background singing *tonight tonight tonight*.

"I spotted you from outside," she says later, when things get quiet, when we're shutting down the bar, "I was having a cigarette and I noticed that jumper of yours. Thought it looked real pretty on ya."

"Thanks," I say, "I found it in the trash."

"Well, it suits you."

"Well, it's old and it's falling apart."

"Hey, you want to meet up with me tomorrow?"

"I can't tomorrow, I have to work. What about next week?"

"I won't be here next week, I gotta go down to New York then I'm back to Australia."

"Okay, if a drink in the afternoon is okay with you then yeah, totally."

"I'm Australian," she says and I say I can tell and she says no, I mean I'll get a drink whenever, my name is Coral.

II

The next day in the afternoon we meet at Ronnie's, another bar a different one and the room is empty except for us, the light streams into the dark room bouncing and slow like a million sea horses floating beneath the slow tide of the ocean, calm, it moves slowly across the floor, warped from the window and warming Coral's feet as we drink three beers each and a shot over a few hours, the room smells sweet, she says, "You clean up nice in the day, don't ya?"

I laugh and say, "I think I clean up pretty good in the night too, don't you?"

"Where you from anyway? You can't be from around here."

"Why not?"

"You're dirty, you're like an Australian but a little shy, a little sad."

"Australians aren't sad?"

"Never met one, nah. You must not have met a lot of Australians."

"You're the first."

"Get out, that's not true."

"I mean, I've met some but never spoke more than a hundred words with one, no."

"Well, we must be up to about a hundred words now, that's a new record isn't it?" but she says "isn't it" like "innit."

She tells me she's only visiting a few days, she finished up a job and went travelling with the money she saved, she'd been to LA and to Texas and to New Orleans and to New York, now she's here in Toronto but is going back to New York in a few days, staying there the rest of the month then heading back to Byron Bay where she lives, where her whole life is, her mom and her dog and beaches stretching out for the rest of your life.

"It feels like I left yesterday," she says, "been gone a month now, got a few weeks left still. It'll pass like an hour, I bet."

And we talk in that bar until I have to leave, I have to go to work, I say let's go to the island tomorrow, you can't come all this way and not go there. She says yes and I go to work that night and it's like I'm standing still now and everything moves around me, moves around her mouth saying yes. The next day Coral tells me she slept last night in a hostel, says, "You could have asked me to stay with you, ya know," and I say, "You can stay with me tonight if you want." Later she stays with me but we don't sleep together, I hold her in bed and she pulls me close like maybe she's been hurt too and quiet and we sleep, a little drunk, a little snow drunk, because that day we go to the island and we stand at the dock where there's a sign pointing to Halifax and a sign pointing to Vancouver which is a stone's throw from Australia, she says, and we share a flask of whisky and everything is quiet, barren of tourist summer stuff and I show her a hidden spot where people have fires sometimes, I know this hidden place because I'd been there with a woman I'd been in love with once, a woman who left me, who I left, and Coral is the first woman since her but I don't ever tell her that because there are some parts of you that are large and are round and are frightening and you don't roll all of that out to anyone for a long time, sometimes never.

We don't leave my apartment all the next day and barely the day after that, only leaving because I go to work and I come home and she's there sleeping in my bed, I slunk in next to her, moving graceful through the morning air like a sea horse in the calm waters deep below the waves, warming her winter feet with my warm body. We make love like all the candles of the world being blown out and we order in food and we watch movies, we drink a bottle of wine and then another bottle of wine and I've never felt so full of love. Or I have felt that love before but it's gone now, that old love, and it's recontextualized and many-layered through the experience of loss. This is happening now, this new big love, the only one now. It's the only thing.

II

A few days later Coral leaves, she has to go to New York to visit with some friends, it was a promise she'd made and she says, "Us Aussies, we don't break promises," joking I think, but a quiet between us then. When I drop her off at the bus station I don't look back because I might ask her to stay and what if she says no and everything we've done, all that love, is ruined. I stay quiet.

She messages me a few hours later and says:

I'm in the USA now, no turning back

and I write back:

do you want to turn back?

and then:

I wanted to ask you to don't go, to stay here with me

and she writes back:

lol you shit

and then:

you should have asked me to stay, I would have stayed with you.
I wanted to.

So it's coming on Christmas and I'm going to New York
because she asks me to come, to spend it with her and her
friends there and I say yes and so here I am, coming to the
USA now, no turning back.

II

The man sitting next to me on the bus doesn't speak
much English and he's young and I have to guide him as
we go through border security, right up to the kiosk, and
I offer to help translate for him and the border guard says
step back, sir, he's fine wait your turn and we both get
through and he smiles at me says, "Merci." I say you're
welcome. I fall asleep and when I wake up all the lights
are coming on in the bus and it's all so sudden and everyone is rushing out now, not yet morning, the flood of cold
from the open bus door and the flooding darkness too and
I walk out into New York shaking now, I shake all the way
to the subway where I go to Central Ave station and on
the way I stop shaking because the subway is warm and
now I'm struggling to stay awake, the calm steady sound
of movement and then I'm there and the sun is peaking
out, I go to a diner called Tina's Restaurant because it's
the only place open and it's all cops and it's all junkies and
it's all hipsters still awake and all of them on cocaine and

it's all me and it's all of us here together, a full cup of coffee the classic kind from the thin tall white cup thick and lipstick-stained.

When I meet with Coral, when the sun comes up and we're sitting at a café near where I'm staying and it's called the Swallow Cafe and I remember when I was a kid I had a friend, a girl named Tina, and she was from New York and she would visit every summer. She stayed in a house on the water and it was her parents' summer house, I visited her often in the summers and I remember every summer there would be a bird always sitting in the same place, on a phone line overlooking the water, on the path I took to visit Tina and it was nice to have something consistent, something always there and it was there every summer until Tina stopped coming to visit and I'd walk past that empty wire sometimes with the ghost of the bird and I wonder what happened to her, it was so long ago I don't remember what she looked like, I don't remember what we did those summers it's all lost now and I tell Coral all of this and I say, "Anyway I think that bird was a swallow."

Coral says, "Do you think we should look her up? Let's all hang out, you, me, and what was her name?"

I say, "I don't remember now, who cares?" and we laugh not because it's funny but because it's just us now, we drink a coffee and we go to where I'm staying, a hotel room I've booked nearby, and we sleep, I sleep through the rest of the morning and I dream a dream of a fire in a secret place and

I'm there and Coral is too and I wake to Coral there with me what better.

II

We're walking through the white winter afternoon of warehouses and men throwing boxes from the backs of trucks, sneakers hanging from phone wires that criss-cross the street like spiderwebs and it's Christmas Eve, everything is quiet here and Coral has some friends who live in a loft nearby, they're having people in, people who have nowhere else to go, she says, so we go there and we bring beer and we bring presents for our hosts, a book we find in the street called *Widow Basquiat* by Jennifer Clement, a bouquet of lavender we find at the only open bodega, a big bottle of wine. A man lets us in, Coral introduces me to him, he lives here his name is Dan, he's also an Australian and he's kind. He introduces me to everyone else. For the rest of the day and night I'll only see Dan laughing with his friend whose name I can't remember, his friend who wears all black and has an accent I can't place, the two of them together sitting in front of a mirror face up like a table dusted white always talking so chatty, moving fast. We eat and we talk and as the sun is setting we all go onto the roof because the sky has turned an otherworldly orange and pink and purple and we take photos of each other and at one point Coral and I are looking down into the street and there's a young couple there in front of a stoop and they're talking and they're nervous and she says, "Do you think he'll kiss her?" and I say, "I don't know, I hope so."

"Do you think they were on a first date just now?"

"On Christmas Eve?"

"Yeah, that's fucking romance right there," and she holds my hand now as we watch them, the sky and everything it enfolds another world entirely.

We stay at her friend's apartment that night, we don't sleep, it's a blur of faces and drinking and everybody has an energy like a sustained forever midnight until the room starts to fill with light and I don't remember much of what was talked about, the country, the world. I remember someone, several people, being vulnerable with me. I remember being vulnerable too. I remember sitting with Coral on a couch, the two of us talking with people like we're one person, like everyone engaging us together as one and in the morning we all exchange presents, all of us still alive and it's Christmas and I don't know these people, just me and her I suppose.

We nap in the day and in the early evening we do the same thing, the same thing from the night before, all of our bodies more emotional, more flung through the world. What even happened then but a lot of words? A lot of moments lost and those faces I can't remember and at the time they were the most important, more important than anything before but now I'm leaving with Coral before the sun comes, in the cold morning we shake through Bushwick our bodies so sensitive now, every light and every sound an assault but we're happy and we go to my hotel room nearby and we rest, we sleep into the afternoon, both of us not dreaming now.

It's Boxing Day, we stay in bed, we start to drink a bottle of wine but it feels bad to be drinking, bad on our bodies, only water. We try to eat but it all makes us nauseous, we stay in bed watching movies, feeling restless, wanting to be outside in the world in New York because we're here so why not but we stay, drunk sick and hungover, thin, barely speaking, slipping in and out of sleep and outside it's snowing and the wind makes a sound like the steady sound of the inside of an airplane coasting high above, flying over the ocean.

||

"We can't stay inside on your last day," Coral says the next morning. "I'm feeling so much better today, let's go out."

"Yeah, I'm feeling a lot better too. What do you want to do?"

"Have you ever been to Coney Island?"

"No, never."

"What? How could you live so close to New York and have never been to Coney Island?"

I laugh and I say, "I don't know, it's just never happened. It's probably pretty closed up today."

"Yeah, it's winter and it's Christmas, probably everything is closed. I came farther than you came, I want to go there. You can't come all this way and not, right?"

She brings me there and the abandon of the place is stark and jarring. A roller coaster ravaged from simple time, hanging by a thread. I remember she holds my hand on the boardwalk and everything is crystalline and it's shining and we're holding hands in this abandoned place, sharing a flask in the cold with this woman and it's so quiet and time stands still now.

One thing I should mention too: in the middle of all the drinking and the drugs and the faces of the party at her friend's apartment Coral tells me about her dog and she says one year to a dog is like seven years to a human which is like seven hundred years to the oldest living tree which is named Methusela, named after Methusela who lived a thousand years or a thousand solar years which is roughly seventy-eight years, she says that we only dream about ninety minutes in sleep but those dreams warp time to their whim to brief moments passing like beams of light or entire lifetimes, isn't that neat? That there are other worlds we hold in our memories through time forever, psychic and subconscious worlds, that we can't understand infinity because there is no point of reference. Another night, a different one, I think the second night we met and she held my hand that night, we walked past a restaurant and we could see inside, an old couple celebrating their fifty-year wedding anniversary and everyone was happy and everyone was saying congratulations and we looked good together, our reflection in the window outside looking in, and it's love again and the universe is one long yawn now, a long yawn from the mouth of a woman waking up in a bed, in the morning, the sun in the sky still burning I suppose, something burning between us.

And that was it. We made love that night for the last time, we slept and we dreamt, we lived an entire lifetime. Something coming back to me. The next day she walked me to my bus after a nice morning of coffee and breakfast and we didn't talk about what we'd done together and we didn't say goodbye, she kissed me lightly and said thank you. I said the same. Then she was gone, nothing else to say and what better way to part than that way, a thank you and gone. She never told me about the man who hurt her, I never mentioned mine. Would things have been different if we'd known? If she'd pulled back the mask and I'd seen the machinations of pain moving like the inside of an ant farm, would I have stayed? If I'd shown her the chasms of my forgetting?

The New Year

IT'S TEN MINUTES TO MIDNIGHT AND THE BAR IS FULL and I'm uncorking bottles of sparkling wine to hand out to everyone, all of us waiting for something new, another chance and Petra says, "They say the way you spend your New Year's Eve is a good indicator for how your whole year will go."

"Who says that?"

"I do."

"Does that always work out for you?"

"I spent my last New Year's Eve crying."

"You cried a lot this year."

"I did. But I'm happy tonight. I'm happy I'm at work, I'm happy to be working with you, that's good."

"Did you see that couple making out in the corner?"

"Of course, everybody has."

"Did you notice she has her hand down his pants?"

And she looks and she laughs and she says, "Oh my god, should we tell them to stop?"

And I say, "Nah. This is how they're spending their New Year's Eve, this is how they want their new year to go. We shouldn't stand in their way," and we're all moving into something new now, all of us together, me and a woman who's happy to be with me and a guy getting fucked.

II

We're there all night, well into the morning and the next day is quiet, I can't sleep. I walk through my neighbourhood early in the afternoon and Toronto is another city now. The city like it is in the quiet hours before the sun when it's dark but it's no longer night, the city where the danger has passed and there's a hum in the streetcar wires like a song, like a light spring shower from every spiderweb of wires tangled above every humming intersection. I think of the people I've loved and the places I've been. I'm in a city drinking itself sick on condos and if everything goes well maybe soon I'll be living in a van, the best I could wish for in the shadow of a million homes worth a million dollars each, the million homes of Toronto. What if I'd stayed in Montreal or Berlin or Taos or anywhere other than this? Would I be anything more if I weren't me but the other man, the man from last night, the man with a hand down his pants? All these strangers coming in and out of my life, gone. What is this love I harbour for them? Will any of this amount to anything when I again meet the eyes that say forever then pass into the next life? Why can't I forget this, as hard as I try. I don't want to die. There's something inside of me I wish would be dead. But once it's died, who would I be. It's part of me now. The thing I wish dead I'm protecting. We might all be micro-organisms, our fate the same as the orchid and the wasp. I'm starting to write again, what you're reading here I write.

II

The first night of the year is always our slowest night but we stay open and I'm the only one willing so I go in to work and I open the bar and I sit reading *Women Who Run with the Wolves* by Clarissa Pinkola Estés and Bill comes in and he sits at the bar.

"Lots of love! Are you excellent?" he says.

"I'm doing okay."

"You look like you're excellent. You look like you're raging."

"What do you mean?"

"I'm raging! I've been editing my book all day, I still don't quite know where it's going to go, the next phase of it. I think I know but I don't because it's all about taking out six pages. When it was about taking out twenty pages they seemed subtle but easier too and now for six pages I go…I'm not really sure. If I take out a three-page poem here and a three-page poem there that changes the facing pages through the whole book. So then that will get readjusted. And with the visual work that's quite a lot of work to do if it destabilizes them. So I'm not sure. I don't have to know yet anyway. But I'm experiencing validation and what's that word… Is it simulacrum? Similarities in tinctures and themes throughout the poems. So all the poems are commenting on each other if you read it that way. But most people don't read books of poems that way so it's just something I'm noticing. It's guiding me in the editing but it may make no difference to the finished book. Some people care about that. Do you?"

"I think everything is interacting, yeah."

"Excellent!"

"What are you writing about?"

"Partly I'm writing about the use of narrative. Do we really need narratives? What are they good for? Do they create more separations? More exclusions than inclusions and acceptances? It's just a question not a conclusion because I don't jump to conclusions, I don't swim a lot, I don't do much jumping. Now I'm swimming a lot. What is this thread? So is this like the lady in the Scots play? Out damn narrative! Out! Out damn thread! I love you thread! We love all the threads. That's what's lovely about writing a novel because there are characters and it is not an extension of oneself. When you're writing a personal poem about grief that's quite long and quite complex then really it's only about me and my friends and the loss that it's talking about. That's an extension of myself to the nth degree, that's very hard to write, I find. As Gertrude Stein said, 'Writing is what you write.'"

"What did you do yesterday?"

"Oh yesterday! Yesterday was New Year's wasn't it? I forgot. It was excellent. Well, first I watched an amazing episode of *Days of Our Lives* while I had lunch. And this one character, she said, 'Sex trumps everything.' And the person she said this to was a much younger guy and he was going with her daughter and she didn't want him to go with her daughter because she wanted her daughter to have a better life than he was able to offer. Why she was able to know that when he was like eighteen and her daughter was eighteen is unknown to me. I don't know what her zeal and her urgency was all about except maybe to make sure her daughter was actually never happy. There's some awful things inside there. So the young man has come to confront the mother to leave him and her daughter alone, that they really love each other. And they get so intense with each other with accusations and threats, they arouse each other's libido and again they get it on, the mother and him. And this will destroy her daughter, who he's in love with. And now of course the mother can blackmail the young guy to stay away from her daughter or she'll tell. If they keep getting it on, someone will find out. Maybe the daughter will find out. But right now she's in California and the mother, last time we saw she was pulling the young guy's T-shirt off and he's been working out."

"Why do you watch that show, Bill?"

"I think I'm interested to see if love is proprietary or if it can be open-minded and if it really is based on possession. And if it is based on possession it's delusional, to be based on that, because it will never be satisfied. People can't possess each other. I've known people who have been very possessional or proprietary. I haven't been very much. So I find it interesting to watch people for which love is proprietary because I've always been puzzled by that. I think I'm more open because I was sick a lot when I was a child and my mother went to spirit when I was young. So I don't expect anything to last. I'm not gloomy about it, I just don't expect it to. Some people with different kinds of early lives think that everything will last and I think they're shocked when it doesn't. Not that I'm also not shocked. I don't know. It doesn't actually make sense. It makes sense but it doesn't hold up. Most people I've been with have been proprietary and I don't at times understand it or actually know what's going on. So I'm looking at Days of Our Lives like it's actually going to teach me something."

"So what did you do after you watched that? Did you do anything special last night?"

"Oh yes, after *Days of Our Lives* I went down the street to get a tea and lately there's this person, she's always sitting at the counter and she's always really nice and I'm always really nice to her, we're nice to each other, it's excellent. There was this dude sitting there with her and he had longer hair like mine and yours, not as long as yours, and he was older like me kind of and he had black-and-white hair and he was explaining to her or narrating, I guess he was saying to her, about the days of 'In-a-Gadda-da-Vida' and the Doors and 'Stairway to Heaven' and he was quoting some of the lines and then he started talking about the acid and I started going, 'Oh microdot?' and he said, 'Microdot!' I said, 'Orange?' and he said, 'Orange!' then we were going, 'Blotter paper?' and we were going like this and she's in between probably you and us and she was happy with all of this and amazed by it, I think she really likes that guy and she's very nice to me as well and then he goes, 'Nights in White Satin?' and I'm going, 'Never reaching the end!' and it was so amazing because that night, me and my friend Sweetheart went to 6 St. Joseph Street and they had a dinner for people that wanted a dinner and it was great and then there was karaoke which I don't really get but I got into it eventually! It was hard to get my head there but I did and someone actually sang 'Nights in White Satin' and I thought, 'I'm going to melt. I'm going to fucking melt.' It was so beautiful to hear that, never reaching the end."

"That's amazing."

"It's so amazing! The threads that run through all this. And when him and me were doing microdot acid was in sixty-seven, sixty-eight, you know what I'm saying? It was so different then, there were no terrorists and shit. I remember I took some to get on a plane. I was going to a reading in Calgary and then I did an interview on CBC with Phyllis Webb and Barrie Nichol sometime around then but I was taking so much acid I don't remember exactly which city it was, I'm guessing it was probably Toronto. I think it was Calgary... Oh but the plane stopped for a break and I just got off the plane and I walked toward the sun on the tarmac, on the runway, and the steward came, I was very stoned, and the steward came in a little truck and took me back to the plane and it wasn't considered unusual, I wasn't jailed for this. Today I would be jailed, you know? So just for these few minutes this person and me were just screaming it all out, how great it was, it was excellent. Life moves so fast. It still really does but...does life move really fast for you? Life itself changes its speed it seems like, doesn't it?"

"It does, yeah."

"Back then I'd only stay in a place for three months. I never was anywhere long enough to go to a funeral of anybody's. There's a lot of things I missed. I don't regret it but I would have liked to have seen more daily life in places. I was very lucky and I just kept moving with it as long as it was going on. I don't know if a phase like that will ever happen again.

I was just thinking about it this morning, I was actually reflecting just a little bit, how wonderful it was, how trustworthy everyone was. I was always travelling. And it was an amazing way to not look at some things in my life. Millions of people live like that, I met a lot of them. They don't stay anywhere more than three months. And very quickly you know everyone that's in the network. You know enough people to know. Then you hear, so and so, this and that, it's all good, you meet them, it's fine. And it's good. Nothing ever went wrong. Well okay, one person, she threw herself off the balcony, that was sort of wrong but she survived and recovered. So it wasn't really wrong. I still believe in magic. As Leonard Cohen said in that poem, 'God is Alive, Magic is Afoot.' Everything will go to spirit but magic. Magic is the spirit. I do believe that. And it's the new year, it's brand new! Magic is afoot! Are you raging?"

The Self Portrait

THERE WAS ONCE, IN LAS VEGAS, I SAT IN THE AIRPORT waiting for a plane to take me anywhere else, anywhere else than where I'd been, and I looked out the window and the window was facing east and the mountains in the distance bore the straight line of light, precise as the cutting of a knife, a line of light from the setting sun behind me to the west separating the light from the dark and I watched that line of light climb to the peak and disappear and the mountains turned purple blue like a bruise and the sky faded orange red like a candle burning low and it happened every day, I thought, this ritual. It happened every day to countless people, all of us indistinguishable if you pulled out and looked at us all together. I wasn't sure what I felt as I bore witness to this incredible beauty in this terrible place that took everything, beat me up, left me in this airport to never come back. I wasn't sure if anything here felt anything toward me. I loved it still I suppose, I was brought here to find something and I didn't know what yet.

Why was I in Las Vegas. Why was I anywhere. I remember once standing at the grave of a man who was buried in the Memphis Zoo, his grave overlooking the tiger pit where small waterfalls fell over the bodies of animals meant for another world. I remember sitting in a hot tub with a Norwegian man in Reykjavik, he was thin with a long beard and he hummed because he couldn't hear and he might have been the oldest thing I'd ever seen, I wasn't sure anything else could ever live that long, and the two of us sat in that water and it was like he was singing for me only and a light snow fell softly on us, just us two. I remember walking through a forest on the east coast and the snow was heavy on the ground and I was sure I was lost and there were small dots of dark red like blood there in the pure white snow, I was sure a bear would find me or a wolf and then that would be that there in the brisk morning of early winter and I came upon an abandoned house, all the windows broken out and I couldn't stand to step inside of it because of the quiet that radiated from the broken walls, there might have been someone upstairs, there was a sound and the sound brought a darkness to the forefront of my mind so I left quietly and I found my way out of the forest and the people in the town that I was in, they spoke to each other as if they weren't surrounded by this mystical darkness, this wild world full of spirits and death. Why was I in any of these places?

I remember back when I was in Montreal Laura asked me something and I remember it still, she asked why are you always up and leaving everywhere and I said because no one ever asks me to stay. I didn't think I'd say that, didn't even know I thought it, but here it came out, as much truth as I'd ever hid from myself. No one ever said: I wish you'd stay here. With me.

Except L did.

Before me, L had said, she'd been through too much. Abusive relationships, bad family life, no stable home ever. She was a runaway like me, she'd never stayed anywhere more than a couple years. She was an outsider everywhere she went. Before me, L had said, she had friends but they weren't really friends, they were people who were convenient. They were unkind, they stole her money and they slept with her partners, they disappeared when things went bad, when she needed them. Before me, L had said, the men and women she dated were at first kind but something always turned, they mistreated her, took advantage of her emotionally, physically, sexually, they made her feel more alone, what was exciting at first became for her a dark and predictable and shallow thing. And she was kind despite all this because some people are born without luck, an abundance of naïveté and trust, a deep kindness that can't be shaken. I felt in many ways that she was my twin.

I didn't know any of this except for what she told me later, long after we met. I also don't know this for sure, she'd never admit it, but when we met I think she wanted out, she wanted out of everything the whole deal, and I think she saw me and she saw one last chance, a buoy in the middle of everything that was crashing all around her. I felt the same about her. I thought she was beautiful but more than that I was happy just sitting next to her, listening, doing nothing. We could have done nothing forever and she knew that and she held on to me like I was all she had, tethered to something, anything. When we were together I barely did anything else but be there and I was happy. I'd never known how that felt. I'd looked for it everywhere.

And she held on hard. I remember once, early on, I was out with a friend and she texted me, "I need you to come home," and I said, "I'm just out with a friend, I'll be home in a couple hours," and she'd moved in with me right away, us living in this tiny room so small you could only fit a twin bed and we had to hold each other just to fit on it, even in the summer when our sweat sealed us together like glue, waking up in the night peeling us both from each other, and anyway she wrote me back and she said, "I'm having trouble, can you come home now?" and that was that. After that one time that I dropped everything and came to her, her at home crying because she felt alone or too much darkness and I calmed her then and everything was okay, after that I came home every time without question. I left work early some days to be with her. I lost a job once at a tech start-up I worked for, in an office at a desk and I hated every minute of it, I lost that job because I left early too many times, because I went to her always. But that was fine. We didn't need money. I needed her.

We really did have no money then. We barely made rent most months, we found ways of eating very little—lots of caffeine, tea to stave off hunger and nausea. Rice and potatoes. I picked up the odd catering job because rich people don't eat either and they're thin and they would leave tables full of food that we all were allowed to take after everything was over, whatever was leftover. Sometimes I let the people I worked with take most of the food because I knew that some of them needed it more. I knew that some people will never know love. I don't remember us ever going to a restaurant. We never went to a soup kitchen or a food drive at that time but thinking back on it I suppose we could have. But again, there were others who needed those things more.

I lost a lot of friends during that time. I didn't have time for them or when I did it caused L so much anxiety that I couldn't bear to see her like that, couldn't bear to see her hurt. I especially lost women, women who were friends of mine. L was a jealous person and that was okay. I would never meet with anyone I'd slept with before her. She found out who those women were and when she saw them, if we passed them in the street or saw them at a party it was like something inside of her shook.

And she was kind and I was happy simply sitting next to her. And why would someone leave that, why would you leave that for any reason.

But something did happen. I still don't understand what. It was like she let go of something inside of herself and she turned into everyone who ever hurt her. All the abuse she'd suffered, she took control of it, she held it in her hands now, she became it. She became them. But she wasn't them. She was her. And she pulled away and she pushed me and she tried to make me leave her. She hurt me. And every time she hurt me she would hold me. Do you know what it's like to find comfort in the arms of the one who hurt you? Do you know what it's like to be willingly drawn into the thing that consumes and repels you?

That was when she left. And she said, "You deserve better." Whatever internal compass I had was broken. No one deserves anything, I told myself then. The universe is chaos. Good things happen to bad people and bad things to good. Everything happens and you move. There's no moving on, no looking back, these things happened and you move. And if I deserved anything it was that I deserved her. Not the her she became but the her I remembered. The her in my head. The her who had loved me. What I deserved was love. But who would love me now.

I only saw her once after everything happened. It was a few years later and she came to my apartment, said a friend had given her my address, could she come in? I said okay. She sat on my couch and I gave her a glass of water because she was swallowing hard and she was looking at her hands and she said she was sorry for everything, she looked me in the eyes then. She said she was sorry and I didn't have to forgive her but she knew she'd hurt me and she was sorry. I said I'd done some things too that were hurtful and I was sorry for those things too. She looked different. Not better, not worse, but different.

And when she got up to leave I wanted to say don't go. I didn't. That was the last time I saw L.

II

It was soon after that that I met Una. Rienne had moved back to Toronto and she invited me to go with her to an art show one night and I said, "I thought you hate art shows," because she had given up on art when she moved out west, had given up on creating anything again.

"I do but I don't know, I think I'm going to start painting again."

"Really?"

"Yeah, I mean, it's still there, it's still there inside me. I just had to let go of it for a while. Like, even when I gave up on painting it was still there inside me."

"What kind of work do you want to make?"

And she said, "I don't know, what kind of question is that."

"Like, do you think you'll paint in the same style you painted before? Or will you learn new techniques? Will you paint new things? What does it mean to start again?"

"That's too much to ask me, I don't know, man. It's just

something I want to do again. I mean, it's not the same as it was, like I'll probably do new things, sure. It's just different now. It has the same feeling but it's different."

There were a lot of people at the show and mostly people were talking, drinking. There were many rooms, it was in a great loft apartment like a maze. I walked down one hall into a room and the room was filled with mirrors and the people there were dancing, their dancing reflected back and forth for eternity and I walked down another hall and there was a room with great green sculptures of people dying all of them knelt down bleeding multicoloured clumped together dry paint from gashes filled with feathers and I found one room where there was no one and it was dim and the walls were black and there were four framed photos all lit each with their own spotlight and they were of people's faces all of them vaguely familiar and vulnerable the lines on their faces so deep and I didn't want to leave the room, I loved them, and later I met the photographer and it was her, Una, and I realized all of the faces were hers and we spoke, there together, and it wasn't long before I let the tightness of my stomach that I'd come to know as the nervous affection that comes before love take hold and I asked her to spend some time with me and she said yes.

II

When I was a teenager there was a boy who said he was my friend and he told me that one of the popular girls at school had a crush on me and I didn't believe him but he insisted and said he was going to ask her out for me. I told him no, don't do that, though deep down something like a voice from a darkened room locked inside of me wanted him to do it, hoping that maybe it was true, maybe the popular girl did like me. I knew, though, it was a lie. I was repellent to girls at that time, they made faces at me like I was someone to pity and ignore and I wanted desperately to be loved, I had no love from myself or anyone else at that time and the boy walked across the cafeteria and he went to the table where all the popular girls sat, about a dozen of them, each of them isolated, each in their own way with their unique and untouchable beauty, and I saw him speaking to her and I saw her listening and I saw all the other girls listening too and then I saw all those girls laugh. They laughed like the world had come to an end, this was it, this was the great joke we'd all been waiting for.

This was not the story I told Una the second time we met, when we were drinking coffee on her front porch and there was a quiet over the city that night and we had talked about a lot of things but at this point she had asked me what I was like as a teenager.

What I did say was, "Being a teenager was hard, I don't know. I wanted badly to get out of the situation I was in and I did that."

"What do you mean?"

"Well, I was unhappy most of the time. I never felt at home

where I was, I felt like there was something else out in the world and it was there only for me."

"Did you ever find that?"

"I don't know, maybe," I said. "What were you like as a teenager?"

"I wasn't like much to be honest."

"Okay, what do you mean?"

"Well, I studied a lot, I didn't have many friends, I didn't have fun, I liked school and I liked cameras and that was about it."

"Did you have boyfriends growing up?"

"No," she said, "I met my ex when I was twenty-one and he was my first."

"But wait, you were only divorced a few months ago."

"That's right."

"So was he the only person you ever slept with?"

"Well, that's just my business isn't it?"

"Well, I'm hoping it becomes my business."

She smiled and said, "Let me take your portrait, the light is really good right now," and she shot me there in the pink light of the sun where we were. Later that night she brought me to an open mic in the little backroom of a bar where people read poetry, they read either their own work or a piece they had chosen that they liked and it wasn't great but she sat next to me and she held on to my arm tight like she was nervous and after all the performers were done and they filed out of the little backroom I asked her if she had brought me here because she had wanted to read something and she said yes but she had been too scared to volunteer and I asked her what she would have read and she opened her phone and she looked up "When You Are Old" by W. B. Yeats and she read it to me there, the two of us, and I thought this is the sexiest thing anyone has ever done, in all the countless days that have gone by and all the hours, no one had experienced what I experienced then and they never would no matter how many more days counted by in the endless stream of endless hours and of days and of people being born and of people dying some of them passing into the next world right now and I kissed her then, there in the small room and she kissed me too.

II

And the days and the hours passed by with a steady and regular ease, her going to work every morning to the office of a magazine where she was a photo editor, I would wake early when she stayed over and I'd make breakfast. Calmly we'd sit over coffee then I'd sleep a little longer after she left, sometimes going to the bar at night. I was working less then, I wanted to stop working nights because I was getting a little older and I was getting a little tired of it all. I made just about enough to get by, she was making a salary. We saw each other maybe three times a week, on the weekend nights I had off, sometimes having dinner on the nights she didn't stay late at work or when she wasn't busy with her own photography practice. When I had free time I'd find myself fussing over what it is I was meant to be doing in this world where the hours seemed to pass by quicker now, now at the age that I was at.

I remember once we went to the island together and it was a fine day, we took photos of each other on the beach in the sun in the bright afternoon bright like an ad in a magazine of people who look just a little too perfect. We were sitting on a pier later when the sun went down and we watched the sun setting together and I wanted her to hold my hand but she didn't, she watched the sun set as we sat there quiet.

Rienne had a studio and I'd go to visit her sometimes. One morning, after Una and I sat quiet over coffee and she went off to work, I got a message from Matt. It said:

just want you to know that me and Nancy are splitting up. it's okay, it's nothing to worry about just thought I'd tell you before you heard it from someone else. love ya bud

I didn't respond, I wasn't sure what there was to say.

I went to see Rienne at her studio. She was working on a big canvas, just taller than her and just about as wide and it was a nude self-portrait but there was something about it that wasn't her. I couldn't figure it out. There was a violence to it. It was tender. One could look at the painting and see her or one could see someone else entirely, it all depended on who looked and when and how they looked too. After we said hi, hello, how are you, all that, I said to Rienne, her back to me focused on her work but listening, "So, I got a strange message this morning."

"Oh?" she said.

"Yeah. It was from Matt."

She didn't turn around. There was a pause as she kept painting. "Was it about him leaving his wife?"

"How did you know?"

"We still talk sometimes. He told me."

"I didn't realize you two still talked."

"Yeah, we didn't talk for a long time, not after what he did. Not after how much he hurt me. I guess when I broke up with Alex we started exchanging light messages. I was still mad at him but I was happy that he was happy, I was happy he had a baby. Did you know he always wanted a kid?"

"I didn't know that."

"Yeah, something about his dad. His dad was a big part of his life, he wanted to be like him I guess."

"So what do you think about all that?"

"Well, I guess he's just doing what he needs to do. I'd like to say that I'm mad at him but I'm kind of not."

"No?"

"Nah, it's his life. I lost my ability to say what's good for him and what's not good for him back when he left me. And even then I had no right I suppose."

"But you care about him still."

"Of course I do. But it's his life, if this makes him happy, well then that's just fine. Just a shame a couple people get caught up in it. I messaged his wife. Ex-wife I guess."

"Wow, what did you say?"

"I told her what happened between him and me, I know he never told her about me. But I let her know that I'd been there, that if she needed anything to be in touch and, you know, you wouldn't guess what she told me."

"What?"

"She said it was fine. She said they agreed to split up, that she appreciated where I was coming from but that there wasn't a lot of support that she needed or him for that matter, as far as she knew. She said they just agreed things would be better for their kid if they weren't together. They're going to work it out that way."

"Hmm. Doesn't sound like Matt."

"Yeah, sounds like a mature person."

She put her paintbrush down and stepped back from the painting, looked at it from far away, studied it, then picked up the brush again. "I still think he's an ass though, he could have done better. Do you think people are capable of changing?"

"I suppose so. I used to be a pretty different person than I am now."

"But I mean, do you think someone is capable of changing who they are, fully. Like, you've learned things and you've experienced things and you act differently than you did but do you think you're capable of changing who you are at your core?"

"I don't know. I suppose so. I mean, I'm pretty much the same person now, at my core, as I was when I was a kid. But if I really focused and spent the time I could probably change all sorts of things about myself. I guess you'd have to change your body, your habits, your patterns of thinking, how you react to things. It would take a lot of effort and it would feel insincere at first but I think it's possible. And sometimes you don't have a choice, shit just happens to you and you go with it."

"But do you think you'd be the same at your core?"

"Do you mean like a soul?"

"Well, I don't think I mean that but I suppose if that's what you want to talk about then yes, you could say I'm talking about a soul."

"You don't think souls exist?"

"Well, look, I think we're an amalgamation of energies that are so disparate that it's a miracle they come together to create what we are. And I think those energies have their own, I don't want to say personalities, but their own nature. They hold something like memory. Like they came from different places with different elements and memories and they're all interacting together. But I don't think that's a soul exactly."

"So what is it?"

"I don't know, man, it's just a mess. It's a mess of experiences and memories and things all coming together and making a mess of each other, which is what we're made of. It shouldn't be there but it is so you deal with it. And anyway, we were talking about Matt."

"Yeah, I guess so. I worry about him is all."

"I worry about him too." Rienne motioned toward the painting and asked, "What do you think of this one?"

"I love it."

"But is it good?"

"What's the difference?"

"What do you mean what's the difference? Loving something doesn't make it good. And something being good doesn't mean you'll love it. You love it, but is it good?"

I didn't have an answer for her. I couldn't tell. I asked her, "What made you want to paint this?"

"Well, I don't think it works that way. I didn't want to paint anything. This morning I was journaling and I couldn't stop writing and thinking about Matt and what happened between us and where he is and where I am now. After he left, I suffered a lot. I might not have shown it. It still hurts. I figure it always will. It'll change but it'll always be there. And I came here with the intent of painting so I did, with that in mind. I don't want to paint my suffering, it's such a cliché, but it was what felt most urgent in me so I started. And here it is. I think it's almost done."

"The painting? Or the suffering?"

"I don't think I'll share this though," she continued, as if she hadn't heard me. "Not with anyone. It feels like maybe it's wrong to do that. I don't know. I don't want to fetishize my suffering. I don't want people to consume it. You know, before I met Matt it felt like everything in the world was telling me I was unworthy of love. I didn't deserve it. They didn't have love so I couldn't have it either. I'd internalized that and I didn't love myself. But then there it was. Someone loved me. I loved someone. I had love inside me. It felt like a rebellion against everything. Fuck the world. I'm worthy of this. And I worshipped it. No one can take that from me. I still feel a fidelity to that love, though it has turned and this is what it has become. Ugly and undignified. Embarrassing. I feel like I've stayed true to love in this way. And like, I'm healing, which is a worthwhile pursuit. This painting is part of it. I'm worth it. Healing is the beautiful face of suffering, which I think this painting is tied to. It's somehow tied to beauty. But anyway no one else gets to see this." Rienne turned her head toward me, her body still facing the canvas. "How's Una?"

"She's good," I said.

"I like her."

"Yeah, me too."

"Do you think we need to be defined by the people we couple up with?"

"What do you mean?"

"I mean, we all seem to reach after love and for whatever reason that love often gets translated not in the love we offer ourselves but the love we offer another person, often monogamy."

"I guess to love yourself is viewed as selfish where loving another is selfless."

"But what about all these people who hurt us? You know, Matt hurt me. What was the name of the one who hurt you? Law? Do you think they really loved us?"

I hadn't thought about L in a long time. I couldn't even say her name. Her true name which now reverberated through my head like a low hum. A car horn sounded just outside, just in the distance, from what sounded like a broken old car. "I don't know," I said, "they sure weren't there when we needed them."

And I left Rienne's studio soon after. I walked through the city and I realized I hadn't done that in a long time, just to walk alone with nowhere to be. I walked past the place where L and I first met, past the house we lived in once, past the place where I realized I'd lost her, where I threw up from the pain that tightened my stomach. All these places seemed new, a new coat of paint, remodelled but haunted still like porcelain around bone marrow where once there was bone.

I remembered once, when I first moved to Toronto, before I met L or Rienne or Matt or Laura or any of the countless people I've met, I worked in a restaurant and I wasn't there long, just washing dishes until I found something better, and I worked with a man whose face I can barely remember, it was so long ago, and we were drinking after work, just the two of us, and he told me, unprovoked, that when he was younger he went to Paris with his then girlfriend.

"Her name was Eliza," he said. "I went back there by myself about ten years later, many years after we'd split up. But Paris became, for me, a ghost town of Eliza."

I asked him what he meant by that and he said everywhere he'd been, there she was. I said I don't understand. "You'll understand someday," he said.

Damn him.

II

"What's most difficult, I think, about losing someone is that they're never really lost. Nobody leaves. Nobody dies. Your relationships, even in absence or death, they never end, they only change."

I said that to Una, those exact words, a few days later while we were lying in bed and it was the morning and it was the hour of the morning just before the only square of direct light of day that entered my room was sliding off my bed like a veil from the head of a bride.

"Are you okay?" she asked me. "You've seemed distracted lately."

"I think I'm okay," I said.

"You think?"

"Yeah, I don't know. I guess I've been thinking lately that I've been in Toronto for a long time."

"You feel like you need a change?"

"Maybe not a change. Maybe a little break."

"Like a vacation?"

"Yeah, kind of."

"What are you trying to tell me?"

"Nothing. I guess, like, I used to travel a lot. I don't really do that anymore. Like, I never took vacations, exactly, I just moved around a lot."

"Do you want to do that again?"

"Maybe."

"Where would you go?"

"I don't know. I've been thinking about Paris."

"Paris is nice."

"Have you been there?"

"No, never. Maybe we can go together."

"I'd like that," I said. "I think I need to go on my own though."

"Oh."

"Is that weird?"

"No," she said, "sorry, I didn't mean to sound upset. It's totally okay. I think you should do that."

"You're not upset?"

"Well, I was for a second there. But honestly, Brad, if you

feel you need to do something by yourself you should. I mean that. And not just this, I mean anything. I'm here with you because you're a good person and I like spending time with you but if you need to do things that don't include me, that's okay. I would never want to hold you back from anything, even if it means you're away from me."

"But what if I did something like this… Okay, hypothetically let's say I went to Paris and I decided I never wanted to come back? What if I started working on a farm and I liked it and thought this is for me, I'll never want to be anywhere else. What if I found something that took me away?"

"I'd be happy for you."

"No way."

"Yes! You know I'd miss you and it would be sad and I'd always have this imagined future in my head of what if things had worked out between us, but that's just what that is, it's an imagined future. You're here now and that makes me happy. If I knew you weren't happy doing this I wouldn't want you to do this. I want you to do what you want to do."

"What do you want to do?"

"I don't know. Honestly I have to go to work soon so I want to shower and I want to drink some coffee and I want to not be late for work. That's what I want to do. And I want to see you later."

"Okay. Well, I'm going to think about it."

"Great," she said. "You should," and she kissed me and she left the room. I heard the bathroom door closing and I heard the squeal of the knobs of the shower turn and I heard the water hit the porcelain of the floor of the tub and I heard her delicate first step into the heat of the water, I heard the water hit her body, I felt the warmth, I heard the low hum of her soft morning voice hum a tune I'd never heard, something reaching into the near future where I may or may not be, somewhere singular and free, a quiet place free from pain and I thought, alone now, rising up and moving toward the morning, she didn't ask me to stay. She didn't say don't go.

Acknowledgements

Thanks to Stephen Thomas.

Thanks to Ashley Obscura.

Thanks to Guillaume Morissette for being a first reader and to Lena Suksi and Aley Waterman for their advice, thanks for their friendship and guidance and hard work.

Thanks also to bill bissett and Noah Goodbaum. Rob Cram & Charlotte Ficek, Chris & Britt Boni. Matt Caudle, Trevor, Jac and Allie Blumas, and Jesse Wick for their support.

This book would not have been possible without funding from the Ontario Arts Council and all the work of those at Book*hug.

Versions of "The American" and "The Coyote" originally appeared in *The Puritan* and *Bad Nudes*, respectively.

.

BRAD CASEY is a writer who currently resides in Toronto. His first book of poetry, *The Idiot on Fire*, was published by Metatron. He has performed his work in Montreal, New York, Los Angeles, Berlin, and Gothenburg. His work has also appeared in *Hobart*, *Vice*, *The Puritan*, *Peach Mag,* and more. This is his first novel.